G000016162

ACKNOWLEDGEMENTS

While some of the following dits and jokes have, in one form or another, inevitably been told over and again on various mess decks, these are interspersed with tales and revelations sent to me by various sailors from around the world, each who claim 'their' dit to be new, genuine and never told before... yeah, of course, mate.

Anywayhow, this is my official way of saying thank you to each and every one of you who has sent, emailed, messaged or otherwise contacted me with a dit, joke, ditty, oddity or a bunch of pure drivel.

B Z, mates

JACK'S
DITS 2

MORE TALES FROM

THE MESS

MORE DITS, MORE JOKES

MORE DITTY'S & MORE ODDITIES

© Paul White 2021

ALL RIGHTS RESERVED.

No part of this publication may be reproduced, distributed, or transmitted in any form or by any means, including photocopying, recording, or other electronic or mechanical methods, without the prior written permission of the publisher, except in the case of brief quotations embodied in critical reviews and certain other non-commercial uses permitted by copyright law.

TOADPUBLISHING@MAIL.COM

DEDICATION

This book is dedicated to my oppos.

Those who became my long-standing friends. Those who were short-lived associates, and those who were fleeting encounters during the hectic, chaotic, seemingly endless life I lived as 'Jack'.

All of you, singularly and collectively, influenced me in some way.

Cheers, shippers

~~FOREWORD~~

FOR'ARD

Foremost, **Jacks Dits 2** is a collection of humorous tales, jokes, quotes, and oddities peculiar to the Royal Navy, particular of the years circa 1950 to the early 1980s, although some leeway is given by the author as to the precise era in which these tales originate.

There is an old adage which states, *'That many a true word hath been spoke in jest'*, and this is true of Jacks Dits, both this and the previous volume, where honest, accurate historical attitudes of our society during such times are recorded within the oft flippant telling's, and the mirth and merriment, of these stories.

Measured against current social trends and political principles, some of the contents of **Jacks Dits 2** may be regarded as racist, sexist and many other 'ist's'. Paul does not hide any of the bigotry, prejudices or discrimination which may have existed during the period these tales are taken. He firmly believes to alter, edit, delete, or otherwise adjust the facts, would interfere and distort the accurate and factual recording of Royal Naval social history. **Something he is not prepared to do.**

If you are easily offended or find views and beliefs held, which may not be in line with your own viewpoint, unacceptable to your sensibilities or you are, in fact, simply a 'Snowflake' or at least identify with one, then **Jacks Dits 2** is not a book you should read as this book honours the true facts of life, it does not attempt to smother them with the distortions of perceived correctness.

As Jack would say...

"Oh...wee...

Don't give a toss for the skipper or the Joss or the Killick or the buffers parteee...

It's half past four and we're off ashore to play the Jack me heartee..."

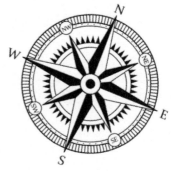

B u s t e r   B r o w n

CPOCK & lifelong Jack me Lad

INTRODUCTION

Jack's Dits 2 – More Tales from the Mess, continues spinning humorous yarns, fables, anecdotes, and jokes which originate in the mess squares and on the decks of Royal Navy ships and shore bases.

Those included here are mainly from the mid-1950s to early the early 1980s, but extended inclusion is made to encompass all the stories told here with.

Continuing from the original *'Jacks Dits – Tall tales from the Mess Deck'*, Jacks Dits 2 mixes more dits and more hilarious jokes, interspersed with a further flurry of ditty's, quotes and oddities which will entertain and amuse, along with evoking fond memories.

Jack, in his wisdom, sought at every opportunity to highlight the differences, abnormalities, oddities and strange traits of body, form and personality, of each and every individual. This was not designed to be to the detriment or exclusion of any person, but a way of inclusion, of acceptance, a passage of rite into the brotherhood of seafarers.

It was an individual's ability to accept and learn to refract, deflect and return insults, offensive statements, slurs and slights which made Jack stronger, founded and strengthened bonds between individuals, messmates, oppos and the Andrew itself.

Anyone not experiencing such close military environments may find difficulty in recognising the strength of the bond formed during such comradeship. The unity, loyalty and solidarity created by such a esprit de corps.

The cutting humour, absurdity, and preposterous farce, which frequently contains obscenities, is regularly sexually explicit and often vulgar is repeated here, in **Jack's Dits 2 – More Tales from the Mess,** as it reflects that bond within the comedy of its content. It is, in a large part, the sharing of such humour between the men who served which made the Royal Navy the best navy in the world.

A navy I was proud to be part of.

Paul White

Ex-R.N.

SPAR-LASH AND THE SPROG

I sent a young sailor in search of a 'Spar Lash' as he was acting like a frigging yappy Jack Russel and wouldn't shut the fuck up.

He needed a distraction, and I needed a bit of peace and quiet.

The skin bumbled around, all over the ship, visiting about every department.

We rang on ahead, on 1mc, so they knew the lad was being wound up.

The sprog came back well over an hour later, thankfully near to the end of our watch so we wouldn't have to listen to his squeaky yammering for too long.

He handed me a lump of metal, some doofah one of the stokers handed him at his last port of call.

I asked him why he had been gone so long and he said no one had one, so they sent him along to the next store, then the next and so on. (Just as planned).

But he seemed chuffed he finally found a Spar-Lash.

I then asked if he knew why such an odd shaped piece of rough metal was called a 'Spar-Lash'?

Of course, he did not, but guessed it was to fix something to a spar.

I said, "Nah mate, your frigging miles off. It's because it does this. Listen."

I made a great show of bowling the lump of metal over the side.

The sprogs jaw dropped.

"Did you hear it Spar-Lash into the oggin?" I asked him.

We pissed our kegs.

A Nut Job

I was married by the time I was 20.

Like most randy matelots, I produced a family at the double, with our third daughter arriving by the time I was 30.

This time my Wife experienced a difficult birth and, after discussions with her and our GP, I decided to do the decent thing and go for the snip... and because I did not want the alternative my wife offered, which was a celibate life.

Anyway, I mentioned the possibility of having the 'op' on the NHS. But this, so it seems, involved a lengthy wait and my wife was not waiting for anything, so I decided to fork out twenty-five quid's worth of my hard-earned beer tokens, simply so I could have it done privately, within days.

A week later, having shaved off down below. I drive to the 'Private Hospital' to have the job done.

I was laying on the surgeon's table when this big, butch nurse walked in. To be honest, she had more stubble on her chin than most three badge OD's with a full set.

Without pausing, this harridan gathers up my meat and two veg in one of her latex-gloved porky palms and, looking at my pristinely plucked penis, says...

"My, you have been a good boy. Now don't worry yourself, this won't hurt a bit."

I think I held my breath the whole time, but she was right, it didn't hurt at all.

After the op, I get a cuppa, courtesy of Private Health Care, before getting back in my car and driving home.

Now, all this driving and being molested by Nurse Porky and her playmates had made me a tad hungry. So, on arrival back at base, I asked the joss what time she would have scran ready. She told me I must wait another hour or so, but because I was a good boy, she would allow me some shore leave so I could grab a couple of wets with my oppos.

Fair enough methinks, and off I trots up to the corner tavern to duly imbibe in some pale nectar.

So, there I am, stood at the bar swinging the lamp for all it's worth when, all of a sudden, the pain hits me with a gut-wrenching thump.

It was like a donkey kicking me straight in the bollocks.

If anyone, especially a lardy sausage fingered nurse, ever tells you the snip does not hurt, they are lying through their back teeth.

Wait until the anaesthetic wears off, it hurts like a bugger and then some.

Of course, my oppos, all being sympathetic types, carry on drinking as they watch me writhe around the floor in agony while discussing the levels of agony they think I'm feeling.

CAPTAIN'S NOTE:

The Duty watch does NOT require a key from stores

SIXTY DAYS DQ's

A poem by 'Uncle Albert'

Long ago and far away

while working for the Queen,

I thought I`d have a spot of leave

so left my submarine.

The crushers came to get me

in the middle of the night,

and as they caught me on the job

I didn`t have that much fight.

They marched me off to Pompey

Where they put me in a cell,

I asked them what was going on

but they wouldn't tell.

I'd just barely settled in

when I got the news,

that I`d been charged and weighed off

with 60 days DQ`s

Next morning bright and early

my kitbag on my back,

I marched in through the gates of hell

There was no turning back.

First I met a nice GI

who showed me to my cell,

I asked him where the toilets were

he said, "just ring the bell."

All day long we rushed about

or sorted out our kit,

The grub was bloody awful

But I was getting fit.

Up at 6 each morning

our routine seemed to be

PT first, then marching,

some marching, then PT

Then after that we had a task

there was no time to mope,

we had to unpick lengths of hemp

And make it into rope.

With bacon on a Wednesday

that was our only meat,

and now and then tomatoes

was a special treat.

Before you knew my time was up

and so, they sent me home,

but no kit fitted any more,

I was all skin and bone.

"Where you been," said her indoors

giving me a kiss.

"You`re looking bloody awful,

have you been on the piss?"

RUN, RABBIT, RUN

A bit of RN history.

Once upon a time...

There were lots of wild bunny rabbits on a big island near Portsmouth, called Whale Island, where many sailors lived happily... okay, this is not a frigging fairy tale.

I'll start again.

Many years back, there were lots of wild rabbits on Whale Island. With permission from the CO of Excellent, you could shoot the little fluffy buggers, providing you did so outside of working hours.

It became customary for shooters leaving the Island to wave a couple of rabbits at the guards and shout 'Rabbits', after which they were waved through the gate without being searched.

Now, Jack being a devious scrounging bastard, soon worked out this was an excellent, (*excuse the pun*) way of getting misappropriated property safely through the gate.

All you needed was a couple of dead rabbits... stuffed with whatever you wanted to smuggle. This misappropriated property soon became known as a '***Rabbit***'.

Such items were considered to have been ***'Rabbited'***.

NOW YOU KNOW... OR MAYBE NOT.

You see, as with all things 'Jack' much of the truth is shrouded in the grey sea mists of mystery... and a ton of bollocks and bullshite.

So, where were we, oh yes.

Once upon a time... in Rowner/Sultan/Collingwood, when Jack had time off, he would take a longboat across to Whale Island to trap a few of those wild rabbits which over-populated the place.

The rabbits were to supplement Jacks meagre rations. *Catering at that time is incomparable to today's luxury victualing.*

Now, back then, it was a 'Naval Overseer' who controlled what work was done on the ship and by whom.

Most work, the official naval work, was, of course, paid for by the Admiralty, but if the ship's captain wanted any work done, which was not on the Admiralty's list, they were negotiated directly with the dockyard fitters and during said negotiations, the payment, or part-payment, was often accepted in the form of rabbits.

Hence the term, **'Rabbit Jobs'**, which was later extended to encompass presents and gifts of various descriptions and not just those 'backhanders' of the 'brown envelope' type.

It is this version of the origination for the term 'Rabbit' which Rick Jolly printed in his book 'Jackspeak'.

However, being printed in a book, even this one, does not make it absolute fact or the truth, as with most of these accounts, they are unrecorded and only passed down in anecdotal form, otherwise known as a **'Dit'**.

Personally, I believe the facts are a combination of both forms of accounts, along with one, or more, similar variations.

The one constant throughout all of the explanations, however, is Whale Island itself and its once abundance of wild rabbits.

This is an unvarying fact in all the reports regarding the origination of the term 'Rabbits' for it to be considered anything less than factual.

THEY SENT ME FOR...

Batteries for the deadlights.

While we are on the subject of Rabbits...

A RABBIT JOKE

A rabbit walked into the 'Mighty Fine' in Pompey and askes the barman for a Pussers Rum and a Cheesy, Hammy, Eggy toastie.

The barman is amazed at seeing a talking rabbit in his bar, but serves the rabbit anyway, who downs his tot and snaffles the butty before leaving.

As it happens... the following night the rabbit returns, asks for a Pussers Rum and another Cheesy, Hammy, Eggy toastie. The barman, now intrigued by the rabbit and the way he has attracted extra drinkers in the pub, gives the rabbit the rum and the toastie for free.

The next night, the Mighty Fine is packed with Matelots. In comes the rabbit and says, 'A Pussers Rum and a Cheesy, Hammy, Eggy toastie," please barman.

The crowd hushed as the barman gives the rabbit his rum and toastie and then burst into applause as the rabbit wolfs them down.

The next night, the word getting around town, the Mighty Fine is packed to the rafters, a shed load of coaches were laid on to bring people into town from all around. The barman is ecstatic, he has taken more money since the rabbit started coming than he did all of last year.

As regular as clockwork, in walks the rabbit and says, "A Pussers Rum and a Cheesy, Hammy, Eggy toastie, please."

The barman says, 'I'm sorry. Mr Rabbit, old mate, old mucker, but we are right out of Cheesy Hammy Eggy toasties."

The rabbit looks aghast.

The crowd has quieted.

The barman clears his throat and says, nervously, "We have some very tasty Cheese and Onion Toasties."

The rabbit looks him in the eye and says, "Would I enjoy one of those?"

The massed customers stand with bated breath, all is ear shatteringly silent.

The barman, with a roguish smile, says, "I am sure you'll love it, Mr Rabbit. I would never suggest something you wouldn't like."

"Ok", says the rabbit, "I'll have a Pussers Rum and try one of your Cheese and Onion Toasties, then."

The pub erupts with glee as the rabbit downs the rum and munchies his way through the toastie.

The rabbit even waved to the crowd as he left, never to be seen again.

One year later...

The Mighty Fine was now an impoverished bar, the barman, who only served 4 drinks this night, 3 of which were his own, calls time. While he is cleaning down he sees a small white form, floating above the bar.

The barman asks, "Who are you?"

The answer is, "I am the ghost of the rabbit who used to frequent this bar."

The barman says, 'I remember you. You made the Mighty Fine famous. You came every night for a Pussers Rum and a Cheesy, Hammy, Eggy toastie. Hundreds of people came to see you every night."

The rabbit says, 'Yes, I know.'

The barman, now reminiscing said, "I remember the last night you came. We didn't have any Cheesy, Hammy, Eggy toasties, so you had a Cheese and Onion toastie instead."

"Yes," said the rabbit, "you promised me I would love it."

"You didn't like it?" questioned the barman.

"I loved it." said the rabbit.

The barman asked," then why did you not come back?"

"I died", said the rabbit.

"Oh no. How?" asked the barman.

After a short pause. The rabbit said, "from Mixin-me-toasties."

ZULU WARRIOR IN MOMBASA

I was stoker off the Triumph working Singer FMU, we were now in Mombasa, working on some frigates, living mainly shoreside in a shithole hotel near Tusks on the main drag.

Across the road from us was a night club. Each evening we would wander across the road to watch the stripper strut her stuff. It turns out she was a nice Brummie girl.

We got on well with the staff at the club and they reserved a table for us near the stage each night.

On our last night, before returning to Singers, we sat at the reserved table and began to enjoy ourselves, ordering more 'Tusker' than usual. We were going to celebrate our last night in style.

At midnight, the lights dimmed, the drums rolled and, as usual, the first few bars of the 'stripper' blasted from loudspeakers.

The club was full of Matelots, more ships arriving the day before, most Jacks we're accompanied by their newly found local female friends.

From the darkness, the spotlight lit up a figure in the centre of the stage. It was not our regular Brummie stripper, she was sitting next to me, but a Scouse stoker dressed in a tutu.

The place fell silent for an instance before Jack getting the joke, started a chorus rendition of Zulu Warrior.

Scouse began divesting himself of his leotard and tutu as the singing grew louder and more raucous. Even our Brummie lass was shouting her head off and clapping.

Unknown to us, Scouse and the stripper had been shagging the whole time we had been in Mombasa and they organised the whole charade with the club's management as a farewell gift to us.

The other sailors did not go unrewarded, our friendly Brummie stripper treating them to the real show a little later.

I wondered what happened to our stripper, maybe she and Scouse are still together?

STICKY GREENS, MOTORBOATING AND THE YAKUZA

I remember when we went to 'Kagoshima'; although this was in 1960, we were the first British ship to visit since the end of the second world war.

Located at the southwestern tip of the island of Kyushu, Kagoshima is the largest city in the prefecture. It is nicknamed the 'Naples of the Eastern world' for its bay location, hot climate, and the imposing stratovolcano, Sakurajima.

It was the first night in port when the four of us went ashore. We didn't know what to expect from the locals. We were warned before going ashore the Japs were still not on the best of terms with the Yanks... for some reason or other.

Getting out of the liberty boat we noticed a woman sitting on the jetty, tit-out, feeding her baby. Oh ho, we thought. This could be promising. *(Note: The attitude towards breastfeeding and bearing breast in public places was a little different back then, particularly for us 'westerners'.)*

The early evening seemed to go by unspectacularly. A few beers, another bar, a few more beers. However, as the night progressed thing became a little more... well, lively.

The four of us stagger into the next bar where, for the first time that night, we find ourselves the attention of some bargirls.

Now, this is more like what Jack was used to.

As expected, the girls asked us to buy them 'champagne', which in these types of bars is simply coloured water, often referred to as 'Sticky Greens' and bought throughout the world by Jack. It's a scam, we know it, they know it, they know we know, they know we know they know... life goes on.

We had been at sea for a while and the old Testosterone was pumping around our nut-sacks, so we got the stickie's in, obliging the girls to sit at the table with us.

One sat next to me and, as any randy matelot would do, I slipped my hand inside her blouse and fondled her bosom, she was reasonably well built for a Jap, who in my experience tend to have smaller appendages.

She seemed happy kissing and canoodling, so I hook one of her puppies out and dive in for a good nipple sucking session.

She laughs, jumps up and goes straight over to the barman, says something in Japanese and he comes out from behind the bar and starts making his way across the room towards me.

I said to me oppo's, "I think I'm in the shit here. Legit if you don't want to be dropped in it too."

They stuck around. I think they were eager to watch the shit being kicked out of me.

The girl arrives back first and plonks herself back in the seat next to me and then hoists both of her tits out, gesturing me to get stuck in.

"What the fukees going on-ee" I said, in my fluent version of Japanese. (*It's amazing what you can learn in a few hours.*)

She nods and smiles, grabbing hold of my head and pulling my head back to her teats... so, okay, I admit I didn't put up much of a fight and soon I was happily moving from left nipple to right nipple and back again.

The barman, who was hovering above us, starts to roar with laughter as he watched me motorboating her boobs. Still pissing his pants, he wanders back to the bar muttering some shite in Japanese.

A short while later the bar doors open and a bunch of locals arrive. The barman jabbers to this group and points towards us. The whole bunch of Japs who, at least in my mind, all began to look like ninjas, or Yakuza, came over to our table, followed by the barman who mimes sucking tits and points to me.

The girl holds her chest out to me, so I do the deed again. As I do, the locals laugh their heads off like a bunch of hyenae. The barman sends over a few beers for our table. It seems we, or I, have become the star attraction of the night.

Then, whenever anyone came into the bar we all, that's the four of us, had to all do the tit sucking/motorboating thing with girls to entertain the patrons. That is every time anyone entered, all night long.

Of course, I suspect we could have left if we wanted, but the locals kept plying our table with beer and whisky. We got pissed as farts, the locals got entertained, the barman got a crowded bar and his till kept ringing. Everyone was happy.

For us, the biggest bonus of the night was, when the bar closed, we got to take the girls to a 'Hotel' for the night, well for a couple of hours anyway.

So why did this happen? It seems, in this part of Japan the men don't give a shit about titties. They think shaking hands is far more intimate, which is why they bow to say hello.

I have no idea if it's like that nowadays, but then it was a matelots dream run... we spent three weeks in harbour.

Wonderful times.

TORQUAY '77

HMS Torquay was a training ship for officers, weapons electrical etc.

Spider Webb was the Killick cook.

Spider was very fond of his drinks and runs ashore with him were legendary and deadly.

This particular dit starts with a run ashore we had on a Saturday in Pompey.

We never went far, mainly just crawling from one bar to the next along the Hard, because Spider reminded us the time spent walking from one pub to another pub was just wasting drinking time.

Anyway, we were duty cooks the next day (Sunday) and Spider was wrecked, I had to cover breakfast for him and was halfway through lunch when he arrives in the galley.

The Torquay had two galleys, one for us mere mortals and one for the officers.

However, on a Sunday all the food was cooked in the main galley so some of the cooks could get a bit of time off. We didn't get that much, believe me.

Spider comes into the galley and asks what's been done.

I tell him it is all under control, the veg is prepped, duff sorted, the meats in the oven, which this Sunday were legs of Pussers Mutton.

Still half pissed, he opens the oven and pulls out a GM tray from the top rack.

As the smell of part-roasted lamb hits him, he throws up the last three pints and the takeaway chicken chow mien from last night's run.

Unperturbed by swamping the roast in puke, he rinses the joints off under the tap and puts them back in the oven, saying to me, *"That top tray of meat is for the wardroom, the bottom two are for us."*

Of course, he is the leading hand, so what can I do but obey his orders?

BZ days.

I'd do it all again.

THE ADMIRAL SAID "YES"

The Admiral has retired, so now it can be told.

From the 4th of June 1948.

This is the war-time story of how I, and my brother, once 'bounced' the Admiral, and not only the Admiral, but his staff, the captains of two ships and, worst offence of all, the Commander-in-Chief of the South Atlantic Station himself.

It was like this.

I was the captain's office writer in the cruiser, in which the Admiral flew his flag when he led some of the famous Malta convoys.

My brother was an ordinary signalman in a corvette. And, when I say ordinary, I mean ordinary, because until his wife became a Wren and put up her hook he had no ambition to advance in the naval scale.

I didn't know where he was, and he didn't know where I was.

Such were the "exigencies" of the Service.

Then, one day, in the summer of 1941, after surviving a noisy trip to Malta, we sailed down South for a respite at Cape Town.

We called to refuel in Freetown and there, sitting in harbour, was my brother's corvette with my brother aboard, experiencing life in the raw with a vengeance.

In the Navy, there are always men in big ships who tire of the 'flannel' and want to be in little ships; and men in little ships who, having had enough of sharing two knives and forks with forty people, long to go to big ships.

So, it wasn't too hard to find someone in the cruiser who would swop a draft with my brother in his corvette.

Whomever he was to be, he needed, of course, to be equal in rate and rank and efficiency and character and service . . . equal, in fact, in almost everything but the colour of the hair and the eyes.

There was not much time in which to do the 'good big brother' act, but at first, things seemed to be going well.

Then the difficulties began to pile up.

Firstly, following the rules and regulations laid down by their Lordships of the Admiralty, the application had to be initiated by the captain of the corvette.

He, after all, was junior to the captain of the cruiser and, although they might be the best of friends at gin time, swopping signalmen was a much different matter.

And the corvette skipper seemed to have no particular desire to be rid of my brother, working, no doubt, on the principle that the known evil, even with signalmen, is better than the unknown.

When that obstacle had been overcome the approval of the Admiral in the cruiser and the approval of the Commander-in-Chief had to be obtained.

It was truly amazing to find how interested captains and admirals could be in what became of you when all the time you thought you were of less importance than the ship's cat.

It was, of course, hopeless. And despite all my pestering of the captain's and admiral's secretaries, whose patience wore thinner and thinner and whose language grew more and more un-officer-like as the day wore on, we sailed away to Cape Town and my brother was left behind.

I remember him telling me later that he rose early to watch us leave harbour and sat on the forecastle, perhaps with tears of anger and disappointment in his eyes, watching his chance of a "big ship" vanish in the morning mist on the horizon.

It seemed too good to be true to call at Freetown again on the way back, if only for a few short hours.

But we did.

Hardly had we dropped anchor than a signal came from the corvette, one junior captain to one senior Captain, asking *"what about swopping these signalmen?"*

Not in those words, of course, but that's what it meant stripped of its naval pomposity.

Within minutes I was active again. The secretaries were pestered once more, signals flashed here and there, papers were exchanged, the man with the longing for little ships packed his bags and drank 'tots' all around the mess.

At the last moment, I almost failed.

The captains had approved, the Admiral was willing.

Even the Commander-in-Chief sent a pleasant little message saying he'd be delighted to grant the wishes of two ordinary signalmen.

But the sea-dutymen were fallen in before I got permission to send off a boat across the harbour to exchange the 'bodies', and it was touch and go whether the Commander would not, with a final word, ruin all the intricate plan.

The commander was human.

The boat pushed off and we were moving out of harbour, when it returned and was hoisted aboard with my brother and his kit inside.

His first words when he touched down were: "How on earth did you do it?"

I was mystified.

"But your old man sent us a signal," I said.

His face was a picture of dismay.

"He didn't! I sent it!"

He hadn't meant to cheat. He was an honest kid.

And how was he to know that our bunting-tosser wouldn't realise the signal was intended from one rating to another, who happened to be his brother, warning him to get cracking?

MF.

RN ret.

GENUINE PIPE

"This morning's tennis team return rackets to the PTI... and BALLS to the Master-at-Arms."

DEEPS AND THE SHIT STICK

It is the early 1960s.

One of Her Majesty's sleek black messengers of death is in drydock at HM Dockyard Pompey.

'Deeps' the Tanky, an able assistant to the Coxswain and oppo of the Leading Chef, is instructed to run an errand to Victory Barracks by the Jimmy.

Resplendent in his battery acid honed No.8 trousers, salt-encrusted steaming boots, off-grey submariner's roll-neck sweater and twisted yellowed cap with tiddy bow dangling over his left eye, Deeps enters Vicky Barracks.

He is strolling across the parade ground, puffing away on a Blue Liner, when he hears the distant call of "that ugly creature there".

Enter into this Gen Dit, a Chief Gunnery Instructor, whose testicles were surely tightly bound with 'Harry Blackers' to obtain the required vocal pitch.

Now, this GI is shaking like a whippet with rickets as he walks, double-time, clenching his pace stick and buttocks, as he clunks across 'his' parade ground in his hobnailed, mirror-polished boots – marching -black.

Deeps, thinking this has nothing to do with him as he is only a visitor to this venerable establishment, amble on regardless. One hand in his pocket, the other casually flicking the ash from his ciggy.

The GI cuts in front of Deeps, blocking his progress and pokes the tip of his pace stick into Deeps chest to make his presence clear.

The Chief eyes Deeps up and down.

Deeps, having met the wrath of many a submarine Chief Stoker before is unfazed by this pristine and polished poser poking him with a pace stick.

The Chief says, in his loudest, tight testicled voice, wanting all the onlookers to witness his wit, "There is a bit of shit on the end of my stick."

Shrugging, Deeps replies, "Not at my end, there's not, Chief".

The result is a chorus of raucous laughter and cheers from the spectators.

A PARTY IN THE GROT

On Hermione, the 4 RM's were in the Gunroom.

On a beer RAS, a lot of it ended up in our cabin as there was loads of space to stow everything.

We were headed into Karachi and had an off the cuff party in the grot.

It had two sinks; the left-hand sink was the nominated heads.

We invited Rick the Can Man, confessing to diverting all his beer. He goes to his office to write-off the crates and brings a bottle of Bacardi back to the party.

A knock on the door as the Captain and Jimmy entered, both were dripping about not getting an invite.

So, we welcomed them, briefing them about the piss sink.

A weird, but brilliant start to a crappy Karachi run.

SEEN ON A RUN ASHORE

On an Athi River highway, the main road to Mombasa, leaving Nairobi

TAKE NOTICE:

WHEN THIS SIGN IS UNDER WATER, THIS ROAD IS IMPASSABLE

MONKEY BUSINESS

A tourist walked into a Portsmouth pet store looking at the animals on display.

While he was there, a commander from HMS Nelson entered and said to the shopkeeper, "I'll take one of those monkeys, please"

The shopkeeper opened the cage and took out a monkey.
He put a collar and leash on the animal and handed it to the officer, saying, "That will be £1,000, please." The officer paid and left with the monkey.

The surprised tourist said to the shopkeeper, "That was a very expensive monkey" back home we can buy a monkey for a few hundred dollars. Why do they cost so much here?"

The shopkeeper answered, "Ah, that was a special Artificer monkey, he can ring for action stations and operate the missile systems of a frigate. That monkey has passed the Navy's Fitness Test and can perform the duties of a Petty Officer with no backchat or complaints. That is what makes him well worth his cost."

The tourist spotted another monkey in a cage. "That one's more expensive. £5,000. What can this one do?" he asked.

"That one," replied the shopkeeper, "is an "Engineer Officer" monkey. It can instruct at all levels of maintenance, supervise repairs of the ship and even do the paperwork. It's a very useful monkey indeed."

The tourist then spied a third monkey. The price tag was an enormous £10,000. The shocked tourist exclaimed, "This one costs more than the other two put together. What in the world can it do?"

"To be quite honest," said the shopkeeper "I've never seen him do anything but drink beer, play with his dick and wind-up the other monkeys, but his documents say he's a Royal Marine."

A STITCH IN TIME

I think it was '74ish. (Tiger)

I sliced through the flap of skin which joins the thumb to the fingers.

Interesting to see inside your own hand.

Anyway, off I toddle, pinching my skin together to stem the blood, to the sickbay.

As it was about time for evening rounds, only the baby doc was on duty... I forget his name.

He got me sat on a chair, arm out on the examination trolly while he set out his stitching gear *(I think docs call it suturing to sound all posh and knowledgeable.)*

He laid out those curved needles, thread, hypodermics, tweezers, dressing and an assortment of medical crap on some sterile paper sheeting.

I asked, "How many stitches will I need?"

He says, "Three or four."

I say, "and how many of them painkilling jabs?"

He answers, "Three or four."
"Why not just stitch me up then? By the time you've jabbed me with the needle three or four times, you may as well just sew me skin together. That's half the number of times you get to stick a needle in me," I say.
(*To clarify, this was not braveness, simply practicality.*)

"Okay, I can do that if it's okay with you?" Baby doc replied.

"Go for it," I said, nodding.

So, he gets the tweezers, threads a needle, and reaches out towards my hand, only now he is shaking like a shitting whippet with distemper.

"What's up?" I ask him.

"It's the first time I've done this on my own."

'Fucking brilliant', I think to myself. Resigned to feeling a lot more pain than I probably needed.
Full of bollox and bravado I said, "Ahh, just get stuck in, mate."

Baby doc shoves the needle in one side of my loose and flappy skin... surprisingly it did not hurt at all, not what I was expecting. Then he pokes the needle through the second bit of skin and pulls the thread through.

Now, for those of you who have watched yourself being stitched together, or indeed practice doing so in a medical fashion, will know the docs have a way of tying a knot without touching the sterile thread.
This is where Baby doc cocked up.
Somehow, he lost the plot and could fashion a knot of any sorts.
I was watching with intent as he pulled the threat taught and then failed to knot it, my skin opening and closing like a bloody accordion.

"Here," I said, getting bored. I took hold of one end of the thread, steadying it whilst he tied it off.
I did this to help him a further three times until I had four neat stitches securing my skin.

Luckily, the Baby doc was just finishing tying off of the last thread when the two and a half ringer doc came in.

I'm not sure if it was his rounds or he came into the sickbay for another reason, but he didn't stay longer than to ask, "Everything alright?" his eyes skipping form me to the Baby doc and back.
.

"Yes, Sir," we said in unison. *(We were lying through our back teeth. Only the doc did not want to say he was nervous and cocking up, and I did not want to drop him in it.)*

As for me. The hand healed perfectly, not a visible scar remains. However, I do hope Baby doc learnt how to suture without help. Goodness knows what would happen if his next patient was unconscious, or bleeding, or both, or...

DIVISIONS AT MERCURY

All were fallen in, outside Leydene house.

It was a bright, sunny Friday afternoon during mid-summer.
The view over the lawn towards the tree-lined grassy avenue was stereotypically 'English'.

This, I am certain, was not lost on the group of Nigerian officers who were on parade with the ship's company.

Captain John Tait is taking the days divisions and, along with his entourage, is carrying out the inspection.

The Captain wanders up and down the lines of men, occasionally stopping to speak to one or to point out an issue with their dress.

He then walks along the line of Nigerian offices who are standing proudly to rigid attention.

Partway along the front rank of these officers, the Captain stops, pointing to a man's absolutely filthy shoes.

The Captain asks the man, "Are they your best shoes, young man?"

The Nigerian Officer replies, "Nah Sir. Not at all, Sir. My best shoes am de blue suede, but I cannot wear dem on divishans, nah."

Behind the Captain, the CPOGI erupts with laughter. The first, and only time, this would even happen... unless you know better?

MALTA, THE NAFFI & AN OLD BAG

I was sat in a bar with a three badge Killick sparker off of the Solebay, a battle class destroyer.
We were all in the Naafi on Manoel Island.

You may know it as HMS Phœnicia or HMS Talbot, it's the same place, Fort Manoel, Marsamxett, Malta.
At that time, a submarine base.

Anyway, the old Killick was entertaining us skins by spinning a string of dits, ensuring, of course, we kept his whistle whet by supplying him with copious amounts of ale.

As the ale flowed, the dits got bawdier, our laughter louder and the language stronger, just as you would expect with a bunch of Jacks out for a good piss-up.

A table away was some toffy nosed woman. What the heck she was doing in 'our' NAFFI we never asked, but as the dits were told the old bag began huffing and puffing, then tut-tut-tutting each time words like bollocks, fanny, fuck or shit were spoken, which is just about the average conversation for sailors in a bar.

She disappeared for a while, clearly going for a slart in the ladies' heads.

On her return, she ensured she passed our table.
As she did, she spoke to the Killick, asking him to *"Keep the bad language down",* to which he replied without stopping to take a breath, *"Sorry love, I thought you'd fucked off."*

That had us all rolling about in hysterics.

I don't know what she did after that but I don't think she was too impressed.

Funny as fuck and the start to a good run.

PUSSERS FANCY FOOTWEAR

Pusser is always changing Jacks uniform. Sometimes for budgetary reasons, sometimes for practical reasons, upgrades in material or, occasionally, to work with new warfare kit.

This was true a while back when the old pattern Tropical Sandals were considered 'not fit for purpose' and new footwear was phased in.

Now, for all the essence out there, I should explain the standard-issue tropical sandals were designed sometime in the 1940s.

Pusser must have purchased around a million pairs of the bloody things, which is why they were still being issued well into the 1990s.

The design of the standard-issue sandals had several cross straps and one central strap which ran from toe to ankle, where another wrapped around the ankle and buckled on the outer side.

This design allowed the (*uncareful*) wearers foot to become sunburned, six bright red raw patches of skin, in a 'window' like pattern.
This, however, was not the primary issue with this footwear.

Although supposed to be leather, the material used was about as pliant and flexible as marine five-ply.
New pairs took some 'breaking in. Around five years would make them wearable without carving great lumps of flesh off the bone when worn.
Many matelots tried to speed up the softening process by soaking them in seawater, boiling them under steam drains, pissing on them in the showers and such, all to no avail.
Most hacked out the central strap, which did not serve any purpose except to pluck out any hairs you may have anywhere on your foot.

Now, where was I?
Oh, yes, we were getting ready for a Med deployment and half the ships company were queuing outside of SLOPS to replace their lost, worn or yellowing tropical uniform.

In the mess D**vy was prancing around showing off his newly issued, upgraded tropical sandals; a rather stylish pair of timberland deck shoes made with baby-arse soft leather.
 What a difference when compared to the ugly clumpers I mention above.

This is when A**dy comes bumbling into the mess.
Now he is a big bloke, a Neanderthal lump of piss and wind.

Once he spies D**vy's new footwear he is aghast.

"What, What are those bloody things?" he says, quivering and pointing.

D**vy explains they are the new tropical sandals which slops are now issuing, but only when your old ones are worn out.

"Fucking right you bloody are," A**dy, says, and digs his old daisy's out from the dusty depths of his locker.
Now, A**dy's had his old sandals for about fifteen years. They are well-aged and now comfortable to wear.
Time and use have conditioned them.
The leather is now as soft as shit and they have moulded themselves to his feet.

However, he attacks them with his rigging set, ripping off the buckles and cutting them to shreds. When he is satisfied, he holds up the tattered remains saying "I would say these are now passed pissing wearing. I'm off to get me new'uns."

He has a large grin plastered over his face. He marches out of the mess, his old sandals under his arm, and off he goes to SLOPS for the exchange to some modern footwear.

Stand easy arrives, NATO standard mugs of tea all around and a bonus, cookie boys have knocked up a bunch of oggies.
Happy days.

Just then the mess door crashes open and A**dy comes storming in, face like a bulldog chewing a wasp and as red as a purple beetroot.

"I do not fucking, bloody believe it. The scabby, crabby fucking bastards." He says, stomping his way to the mess square.

We all stop, cups of tea and freshly baked oggies suspended in mid-air on their way to our lips.

"What's up with you?" one brave lad chances.
"These. These fucking fuckers," A**dy says, chucking a brand-new pair of 1940s issue Pussers sandals onto the mess table.

Several of my messmates almost choked as they pissed themselves laughing.
I almost shat me kegs and fell on the deck, as did a dozen others.
We were unable to speak for laughing our heads off.

It turns out SLOPS were only issuing the new footwear once they ran out of original stock.
Now, most of us, sizes eight, nine, ten were fine, but A**dy, with his huge size twelve plates of meat, would need to wait until Pussers stock diminished, which one Dusty estimated would be in around fourteen years, although I am sure he was just winding A**dy up.

We had a great deployment with some magical runs ashore, most of which were particularly memorable as, each time we stepped ashore, A**dy was there, Elastoplasts patching up his bleeding, blistered feet from the constant rubbing of his brand new 1940s Pussers sandals.

AN OLD DEVONPORT POEM

This is believed to have been written in the 1930s, if you know the author's name could you let me know?

Notes:

A copy of this old poem can be seen on the wall of The Magnet public house in Albany Street.

- *The Magnet was once called The Boot Inn (and Albany Street was once Boot Lane).*
- *For many years, the landlady of The Boot was commonly called 'Ma Boot' and is referenced in the poem as good old Mother.*
- *Jago's Mansion was a pre-WWII nickname for Drake Barracks, fondly named after one of the Warrant Officers.*
- *A good run ashore for sailors was a pint in every public house that stood alongside the dockyard wall, which in pre-war Devonport was plenty.*
- *The Free State was once a nickname of The Fleet Club.*

Come, gallant men of Devonport, your duty will not wait
On tiddley suits and shore-going boots, and muster nigh the gate.

Leave out your starboard fenders and half head one and all,
To South, to North, we'll sally forth, along the Dockyard Wall.

We'll start from Jago's Mansions, men, before we go beserk,
Where deep inside the stanchions hide and D7R men lurk.
But the 'Duty Watch' is calling, so fall in short and tall,
We'll sink a quart afore we start, along the Dockyard Wall.

But up the hill, we sail me lads and down to Albert Gate,
For Plymouth Ales, the "Prince of Wales", by now we're feeling great.
Heigh-ho! The good old "keppels", a certain port 'o call,
To feast and dine on apple wine, outside the Dockyard Wall.

Now tread your measures softly lads and shed a beery tear,
As you guide your feet through Williams Street, for the pubs of yesteryear.
'Spare Boiler', 'Standard','Morice Town Vaults', and those beyond recall,
They stood the test in line abreast, beside the Dockyard Wall.

Across the Ferry Road, me boys, to Devonport Park we steam,
Where tall and straight, the Gunwharf Gate, is on our starboard beam.
A noggin in the 'Marlborough', and as we onward crawl,
We spy once more the 'Fleet Club' door, beside the Dockyard Wall.

Oh, open up those portals wide, the 'Free State' on the hill,
Beneath whose eyes the Tamar lies and Torpoint calm and still,
Where first Dogwatchmen muster, upon the eight-bell call,

To take good cheer, with wine and beer, beside the Dockyard Wall.

But forward men through Morice Square, the 'Lord Hood' stands upright,
The 'Cambridge Arms', the 'Standards' charms, then downhill thro' the night,
'Swans Inn', 'Steam Packet', brothers, and that's North Corners haul,
A pint in each, and then we reach the end of North Yard Wall.

Yet fear not lads, the South Yard Wall, is looming up once more
It upward glides, then swerves and slides, around the 'Boots Inn's' door,
Three Cheers, for good old Mother, the doyenne of 'em all,
Who's always been the Devonport Queen and Mistress of the Wall.

But Devonport Market clock has chimed, the hour is growing late,
The 'Ark Royal's bar is not too far, beyond the Fore Street Gate,
The 'Brown Bear', 'Chapel', 'Beresford', are all good ports o' call,
Still have no fear and sup your beer, there's more beside the Wall.

The 'Bristol Castle', 'Queen & Connie', the 'New Pier' round the bend,
Then on we rode to Mutton Cove, our journey at an end,
And there's King Billy's statue and so lads, one and all,
To South, to North, we've journeyed forth... Three cheers for the Dockyard Wall.

*Putting
Dhoby dust in The Triton fountain,
Floriana is good fun···*

So says a 'my oppo'

STREAKING

I was bosuns mate on the Cherry B in '75.

She was in the basin getting repaired after her major engine room fire.
We were temporarily accommodated in Drake.

It was a Friday, I came off the morning watch but couldn't go back to my scratcher because of rounds, so me and the QM decide to fuck off to the Avondale for a DTS.

It was a blank week, so we needed to go slow supping our pints.

I pop 50p into the bandit and bingo, the fucking thing spat out a ton of dosh, so we went on the rum.

I can't remember getting back to Drake but woke up bollocky buff in the NAAFI automat.

I suppose I did a bit of sleepwalking. Now, having gone walkies I needed to get back to the block, so I ran the 'wrong way' through the shop, which got the ladies screaming at me for being a perv, as all I am wearing is my flip flops.

I hear whistles blowing from the barrack guard, so I make billy big steps all the way to Grenville Block.
Next thing I know, I wake up - again - but this time I'm in a bath, freezing me bollocks off.

Thankfully, I escaped the crushers and thought the whole thing was a dream; until I went for scran and every fucker stood and clapped.

I just wish I had a bigger cock. I don't think I would have been half as embarrassed with a donkey knob swinging between my knees instead of a fisherman's worm flapping around.

Just saying.

THE AFGHAN COAT

Have to admit, I bought a cocky watch in Singers.

Thing is, the 'cocky' must have been a healthy little bugger because it was still going a year later when we arrived in Istanbul.

I was wandering around that massive indoor market by the mosque when my eye caught the sight of an Afghan coat.

Now, for you young'uns, an Afghan coat has more to do with the dog breed than the country.

I shall explain.

In the late 60s and into the 70s sheepskin coats were a 'thing'.

Now, your standard sheepskin coats, think 'Del Boy - Only Fools and Horses - were fine for spivs and football managers, but a bit OTT for those with a more liberal outlook on life, such as hippies and the like.

Enter the Afghan coat.

This coat was, in many ways, very much like a sheepskin, in as much as it was animal skin with a furry, wool inner lining.

Only no one said what creature these Afghan coats were made from, although 'Fatima' or Camel leather was the most common. Most Afghan coats were enhanced by the addition of embroidered patterns, seemingly randomly plastered over the coat, hence their favour with the Hippie culture.

Lesson given, now on with the dit...

I traded my year-old cocky watch, along with a few extra quid, for one of these Afghan coats of dubious origin from a market trader in the souk.

When I sobered up, which was the following afternoon, I found the coat was infested with the thousand flees which should have been happily playing around in some sultan's camel's arsehole.

The coat was then well sealed into a bag full of crab powder and bound with reels of harry blackers, so nothing could escape until I took it off the ship and unwrapped it, once we arrived home

.

Even though I am sure the liberal dosing of flee powder and crab killer annihilated every possible living beastie on that coat, I never wore it.

I did however give it away as a birthday gift.

Well, I'm not that stupid.

. . .And now ladies and gentlemen, our naval friend will render a stirring saga of the frozen north entitled: 'Eskimo Nell'."

A BUGIS STREET TALE

I recall a particularly memorable run ashore down Bugis Street in 1977.
I was on Tiger, group six deployment.

The night was a 'normal' night down the street; noisy, beer flowing, food being scoffed, chatter interspersed with bursts of raucous laughter.
The occasional shout momentarily raised voices of a mini disagreement. All the while, the Kathoey's scamming Jack for 'Stick Greenies'.
Waiters ran back and forth amongst this hoard of people with food and drinks, each establishments' tables identified by differing colour cloths, chairs or parasols.

Strings of electrical cable, many with exposed wires, crisscrossed the road with thousands of lightbulbs hanging from them, twinkling as they shed a yellowy glow on those gathered below.
The scent of oriental cooking, of roast duck, of stir-fried prawns and wok tossed noodles, mingled with Tiger beer, Singapore Slings and John Collins.

Soon, it was time for the Dance of the Flaming Arseholes.

All was going well, simply another night down the Boogie Strasser... then it all kicked off when someone, allegedly a Bootneck off the Ghurkha, chucked a bottle at the OD's entertaining us from the flat roof of the brick shithouse.
Now, the tossing of the odd bottle, full or empty, was not an unusual occurrence.
Most times the dickhead who threw it was admonished by his oppos and life flowed calmly along without most of those gathered even noticing this ripple of idiocy.

However, tonight, for some unknown reason, that calmness did not appear. Maybe Buddha was having a night off... whatever... tonight the entire street erupted into a mass brawl.

From the centre point, the wave of violence spread out, like a shockwave flowing the entire length of the street.

Not wanting to be part of the trouble, I, along with my motley entourage, sloped off into the shadows and took refuge down one of the alleys off the main square.

It was here we found the local Singers Police, sheltering from the riot.
The Local Police were happy to allow the fighting to subside and wait for the main Police Force to wade in, swinging their batons, cracking heads and kicking the shit out of everyone not in a Police uniform, before they sidled out of the alleyway and began to assist the main Police Force arrests the incapable and help the medics collect the injured.

We silently slipped from the darkness of the alley on the heels of the Local Police, before making our way back to the ship.

The following morning, the local newspaper ran a story about 'The Biggest Fight in Bugis Street History'.

I can report that it was a genuine story, but you *'had to be there'* to appreciate it 'properly'.

Great times, happy days.

THEY SENT ME FOR...

A replacement glow-worm for ADR

A DIAMOND GAME OF FOOTBALL

Tiger cubs was the name of our ships under eighteens football team.

We were visiting South Africa and, at the time of this dit, were docked in Cape Town.

That morning, off we go, all gung-ho, ready to play a match against DeBeers, the diamond merchants.

We stuffed them, the score was something silly, (*I lost count*), to nil.

After the game, we all got together in their sports club bar for a few bevvies and this is where they present us with a quarter carat diamond as a trophy of our win.

A great time was had by all until, reluctantly, we had to get on the tilly and head back, so we arrived back on the ship by midnight, under 18's, hence Cinderella leave, even for the all-conquering, mighty Tiger cubs.

On the way back I decided it was an appropriate time for a rendition of Zulu Warrior, which was received with great cheer, only the bastards found it amusing to ditch my divested number ones out of the bus, through the small slit windows.

I arrived on board to collect my station card dressed only in my cap, shitnicks and white canvas shoes.

All told, it was a great run ashore. **BUT**... a dit would not be a dit without a point.

You see... that quarter carat diamond, the one given to us from DeBeers... it was in the pocket of my number one tiddly suit, the same tiddly suit my oppos found hilarious when they ditched it from the bus by ramming it through the window.

Of course, my number ones and the quarter carat diamond were never seen again... not by any of us, anyway.

ODE TO THE TOT

Anonymous

There once was a time in H.M. Ships,
When the magic hour had come,
The leading hands of every mess
Prepared to collect the rum.

The smell of Jamaica filled the air
As the ritual began
A daily tot of Nelson's Blood
Was a favourite to every man.

When the Rum Bosun stood, his measure poised
To serve every man his tot.
Two fingers always in the 'cup '
Making sure the 'Queen 'got her lot.'

The 'ticker off' was there, of course,
His pencil at the ready,
With a sipper given from each man's tot
His hand was no longer steady.

The rum rat sat, his eyes aglow
His whiskers twitching well
He liked his rum so much it seems
He could get pissed on the smell.

Sometimes the tots were passed around
As each man paid his debts
Favour, rubber, game of crib
Could cost a couple of wets.

Then came the time to sup the ' Queens '
"God Bless Her "was the toast,
A watchful eye, as each man supped.
So, the Rum Bosun got the most.

Once the rum had been consumed
And nothing left to pour;
The dits began, as the 'Grog' took charge,
Of favourite runs ashore.

A feed, a fight, a couple of pints
Was part of a run ashore.
A game of darts was in there too
Then all night with a Pompey Lill.

No longer though, does the scent of rum
Pervade her Majesty's boats.
No more to sup Lord Nelson's Blood
And give the Queen her toasts.

So, to all who drank Lord Nelson's Blood
And heard the Klaxon's blast,
May old shipmates meet and share a wet
While Spinning dits of the good times passed.

A toast then to Horatio
And another to the Queen.
And may we all, wherever we are
Remember where we've been.

CAPTAIN'S NOTE:

The Liberty Boat does NOT require a pair of oars.

AIR HOSES AND MARS BARS

On HMS Ardent.

The chief stoker sent a JMEM to get some air hose from the stores.
The junior returned sometime later, clutching three Mars bars.

The chief kindly expressed his thoughts, using as few expletives as any chief stoker might, as he enquired of the young JMEM why he was delivering three Mars bars.

The JMEM replied innocently...

It seems the NAFFI did not have any Aero's, so he used his nogging and, rather than return empty-handed, bought Mars bars as substitutes.

I'll leave the rest to your imagination.

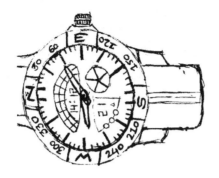

MY THIRTY QUID SEIKO

As a young and very green baby sailor, I was on Ark Royal, my first seagoing draft.

We had done the 'Med' and were visiting Gib on the way home.

As every hairy arsed sailor had a Seiko watch, I decided I 'needed' one too.

I bought one ashore, the first night in dock.

Luckily, I did not have to go to a shop and pay full price, as a couple of locals were selling these watches outside of the bar.

I was well chuffed. I bartered like a 'Trotter' from Only Fools and Horses and bagged myself a magnificent example, for the knockdown price of £30.

A few days later and customs come aboard before we entered Guzz.

You know the routine, the customs guys behind mess tables in the upper hangar.

My turn at the table goes something like this.

Customs man. "Anything to declare?"

Me. "Only this watch", I say. dangling it before his face.

Customs man. "Haha, how much did you pay for this, £2?"

Me. (Getting Irate), "I paid £30 for that."

Customs man. "Are you sure? Looks like a two quidder to me."

Me. (Really annoyed now), "I paid £30 for it and that's a bargain. It's worth much more."

I hear the Reggie, who is leaning against the bulkhead behind me, begin to laugh.

Custom Man. "Okay, If you say so, Jack. That will be £6.50 Import duty."

I paid, turned about and walked away. As I did the reality kicked in.

What a Fucking idiot I was. Customs man was trying to give me a free pass.

But that's not the end of the day.

That evening I was on leave, so took myself off for a good old dhobi; Shave, shampoo, shower, foo-foo dust, splash it all over, the lot.

I forgot about the watch.

First, I noticed it steamed up. I couldn't see the time through the glass.

My old Timex, the one lingering in my locker, never did that.

I took the watch off to find my wrist turning green where it had been.

An hour later the condensation inside the glass had gone, letting me see both the main hands had fallen off, leaving the second hand to sweep around the dial uninterrupted.

FFS.

I had just given HM Customs £6.50 for the pleasure, and let me say, back then I could have a nights piss-up on Union Street and a Ruby Murray for a fiver, so this was big bucks were talking about.

Anyone else been as STUPID as me?

GEN DIT?

The old three badge stoker came into the mess for stand easy.

He looked in the fridge and, on seeing his cherished can of orange Fanta had disappeared he said,

"Well tickle my starboard bollock, some fucker has scuppered me goffer."

A HIGHLAND FLING AT THE BRITANNIA CLUB

I don't know if you are familiar with the Britannia Club on Beach Road in Singers?

In the club, the dining room and the bar are, or at least were at the time of this, um, 'incident', upstairs, including the balcony which overlooked the swimming pool.

It was not hard for a person to imagine legging it off the balcony and 'top bombing' into the pool below.

I think we all must have thought about doing it at some time, as there were so many stories about those who tried, most didn't make the distance, which was much further than it looked from up top, and they ended up crashing into the poolside, causing themselves some horrific injuries.

It would take a very brave, or a very stupid person to attempt the jump.

I was not one of those people.

I am a bit of a coward and allergic to pain.

Anyway, on my dit...

One day I was sitting on the aforementioned balcony, I think it was around 1600 hrs.

I was nearing the end of that days DTS, so was as full to the gunwales of John Collins. Then a load of foreign-sounding army types come wandering into the bar... wearing fucking skirts.

Normally, I would not have said a word, but the John Collins in me had other ideas and soon I was spouting a ton of shite towards these skirt-wearing pongos.

My mistake.

I found out these fine upstanding men were members of a Scottish regiment, the Argyles if I recall correctly. They were on route from good old Blighty to Honky Fid, courtesy of Crabfat Airways.

However, it turns out the RAF shafted the Jocks by supplying a shite airplane that kept breaking down. In fact, it had done so, so many times, it took the Argyles five bone-shaking days to get just as far as Singers.

Even then, their buggered budgie was in Changi, allegedly being 'serviced'.

Needless to say, but I will say it anyway, the Jocks were not in the best frame of mind, being a bit tired and a bit more 'fucking irritable', due to lack of shuteye and... it seems their clean kit was still aboard the knacked boneshaker in the Changi hanger, so the Jocks all smelled like a pair of those proverbial whores knickers.

In an attempt to break the total balls-up of the flight, the Kilt swingers came into the Britannia Club for some air-con (*refrigerated air*), and an icy cold bevvy or two, only to be met by a half-pissed stroppy matelot taking the piss out of their revered uniform.

To give these Highland fellows their due, it is amazing what one man can learn from meeting a group of other military personnel.

That day I learnt how to fly, without an airplane or any wings.

They showed me how a man can fly so fast, so high, and so far, he could land smack bang in the centre of the Britannia Club pool, without coming anywhere near those nasty concrete edges.

I swear I still have an imprint of a size 11 hobnail boot on my backside after all these years.

LANDING

Aircraft approaching RNAS Lossiemouth

Receives weather report from the tower.

Report - "Vertical Visibility ZERO"

Reply - "Is that Feet or Metres?"

A TUPPENCE HA'PENNY RUN ASHORE

We'd been in Piraeus for a couple of weeks, the entire ship's company were low on beer tokens as payday was still somewhere over the horizon.

I was down to my last few Drachma, as were me oppos. Looks like it was going to be a miserable night onboard until someone suggested getting some fags and flogging them ashore to fund our run.

I was a non-smoker and hadn't traded in this month's stamps, so had the full issue of six lingering in the back of my wallet.

An hour later, six of us are legging it down the gangway, each clutching a carton of blueliners ready to sell and fund our night.

It did not take long to find buyers and fill our pockets full of cash, after which we made a beeline for the less salubrious area of Piraeus, after all, that was where the best bars were.

I must say we had a corking night but even six cartons of fags cannot support six hairy arsed sailors until the early hours, so we found ourselves making our way back to the harbour a lot earlier than we wanted.

Passing through the old seaport, on our way to the newer, larger harbour where our ship was berthed, we stuck up a conversation with a couple of very delightful local ladies.

It seems they were willing to spend the rest of the night with us, for a few klebbies each, of course.

Gathering around, we checked what monies we had left. Between us, it came to around three Drachma all told. Not enough for one of us, let alone six, to sleep in a local bordello, less alone a more grandiose establishment.

As it happens, I was wearing a Burberry over my tropic whites and, only because I was pissed as a fart, offered to sell my Burberry to a local to raise enough cash to pay for us all. (*'It'* was *relatively cheap in those days.)*

The lads all thought it was a great idea and chorused how they would all chip-in once we were back at sea so I could buy a replacement coat.

After a bit of haggling with several taxi drivers, we settled on the grand sum of four Yankee dollars, a hefty sum back in those days for half a dozen pissed up Jacks, whose ship was sailing on the morning tide.

So, I take the four dollars, slip it into my pocket and then decide to carry on haggling with the driver, wanting to see if I could squeeze another few spondalokies from his greasy mitts by opening my Burberry, flashing the lining, showing him it was a genuine high-quality overcoat.

After a bit of to-ing and fro-ing, it was obvious nothing more would be forthcoming, so rather reluctantly I handed over the coat to the driver.

We then headed off, with our arms around the waists of the delectable girls, to find the den of inequity where we would be spending an 'all-nighter', or at least the next few hours anyway.

Once a suitable establishment was selected, off we go 'upstairs' to engage in deep conversation and an exchange of wit and humour with our newly gained female friends.

One of the guys decided against accompanying any young lady upstairs and decided to settle on a couch in the lounge and sup a bottle of vino.

"Get stuck in, mate," I says, "fill your boots, we're loaded, just book it up."

The rest of the night passed a bit too quickly. None of us got any sleep, of course, we were all so involved communicating, on an intellectual level, with the girls.

The fact they could not speak more than a few words of English, or we could not speak one word of Greek necessitated with us communicating with touch and body language, a sort of holistic braille.

Anyways, around seven hundred hours, we are ushered out of the rooms and into the main lounge, where our friend was sucking the last dregs from a bottle of hooch. We were served cups of piping hot, rich, thick Greek coffee.

I must say, the coffee was a welcome at that time in the morning. During the drinking of the said beverage, the proprietor asks for us to pay.

He wanted his spondoolkies, his drachmas, or, in our case the promised American dollars.

No.6 trousers, for those who remember, only had one pocket. The one I dipped my hand in and brought out exactly nothing.

I looked around and ask, "Which one of you twats is pissing about?"

I am met by blank stares and a bunch of shrugs.

The manager is looking a little disgruntled at the delay.

I double-checked the little pocket of my pussers money belt to find the grand-total of two shiny pennies and one shiny ha'penny.

Thinking on my feet, I put on a great show of lifting these coins from my belt and, with a flourish, handed them to the manager.

He looks at these strange coins and says something unintelligible, which I took to mean "What the fuck is this?"

Without hesitating, I say, "It's two and a half English Pounds and don't be running off with it all. I want my change."

Now, all of a sudden, the Greek thinks he's got the upper hand and is going to see me off for every bit of dosh he has in his hands

I play along, whinging I should have some change from my two and a half English Pounds. The manager or landlord or whatever he was, was now backing away and laughing, knowing he had my dosh in his sticky mitts, I would not be seeing a single Drachma in change.

My mates bundled me out of the building as fast as they can without causing suspicion and. once around the corner, we leg it down the road as fast as we can bloody well run, in case the landlord sussed out Pennies are not Pounds.

We're still pissing ourselves laughing as we stumbled up the gangway.

To tie this dit up, you may be wondering, or not, what happened to the four American Dollars I sold my Burberry for?

So was I... until it came to me.

You see, once the sale of said coat was agreed, I pocketed the Yankee dollars. After which I decided to show him what good quality a Pussers coat was by flashing the lining, hoping to wrangle a few more klebbies from his tight fist.

As soon as it was clear there would be no further funds coming my way, I took the coat off and gave it to the driver, including giving him back the four dollars he just gave me, which were in the right-hand pocket.

No wonder the driver was laughing and waving as he drove away. The prat.

As everyone was as pissed at the time, not one of us clocked onto the fact, which is why, for the rest of the night we acted as if we were loaded, including charging five all-night rooms and a few bottles of beer and wine to our 'Account'.

Back as sea, the lads kept their promise, chipping in to get me a new Burberry from slops, so all in all the nigh cost me tuppence ha'penny.

I think that is the cheapest run ashore ever... unless you know better?

(I would have loved to have witnessed the managers face when he took his 'Two and a Half English Pound's' to the bank.)

"QUIS ERIPIET DENTES"
(WHO WILL DRAW MY TEETH?)

BLUE MOVIES AND A GRASS

We arrived in the port of Hull from Copenhagen when there was a 'porn crisis' onboard.

It started when an MEM was caught with drugs in his locker, where they (*the Reggies*) also found some porn movies.

When asked about these films the MEM said they belong to the Jack Dustys, and the Dustys showed them in the forward messes while he did showings in the aft end.

The reason for the split in the showings of the various messes was the "Dustys" projector was broken, so, in return for the loan of the MEMs projector, he got the arse end franchise. The cost per head, per blue film show, was twenty pence.

On one occasion in the chef's mess, which, by the way, was opposite Reggie's office, the show was well underway when the catering officer (*Sub-Lieutenant*) waltzed in, did a quick double-take, about turned and disappeared at the double along the passageway back to whence he came.

Hats off to him. He could have dropped the entire mess in the shit.

Now, where was I? Oh yes. The MEMs squealing resulting in killicks of messes and some presidents of messes (*Senior rates*) getting skippers table and fines.

You may be thinking the 'blue-ies' were purchased from Copenhagen, but you would be wrong. The movies were bought out of the Dusty's mess funds before sailing on this commission.

And yes, mess funds are highly illegal, although I don't know of a single mess that did not have them.

How do I know all this? Simple.

I was the Jack Dusty who made the deal with the MEM for the sharing of the movie shows.

I flew off with the Squadron (826), as I was going on draft directly after my leave. Whilst on leave, the NSB (*Naval Specials Branch*) paid me a house call, accompanied by the local PC Plod.

They wanted to know what I knew about the MEM and his drugs. I knew absolutely nothing about that.

Then the porn thing came up. I knew the MEM had grassed on me and expected some others may have mentioned me showing, or at least being present when the films were shown in their messes.

I lost a couple of badges but kept my hook, thanks to the Jossman who put in a good word.

The MEM went to Colchester before being discharged, or so I believe.

I remember the News of the World getting a sniff of the 'scandal'.

They also wrote about a Naval Padre who had to view the evidence by watching the porn films on behalf of the military police. I think it must have been the Church of Jockland padre, Father Brown.

I often wonder who he invited around to watch them with him? My guess is he charged far more than 20p for a seat at his shows.

ACCORDING TO OUR GI

She had a face like

"A bulldog licking shit off a thistle"

A LAUD FOR SALLY TUCKER

There's a dirty little shithouse, to the north of Waterloo,
And another for the ladies further down.
They were run by Sally Tucker, for a shilling you could fuck her,
And sleep with her for half a crown.

She was called Sally Tucker by the men who used to fuck her,
But her real name was Tuloola Johnson Black.,
And when it came to screwing, she knew what she was doing,
And earned a pretty penny on her back.

By the colour of her britches, she was the dirtiest of bitches,
For she never seemed to give the buggers a wash.
But the smell from her vagina was more infinitely finer,
Than any rum or gin or orange squash.
One day she had a ride, with a sailor from the Clyde,

And she wondered why he held her very close,
But when he finished screwing, she knew what he'd been doing,
For he'd left her with a good and proper dose.

She gave it to her father, who gave it to her mother,
Who gave it to the Reverend John Brown.
Who gave it to a cousin, who gave it to a dozen,
And now its halfway round the town.

Now there's a sailor up in Glasgee, that's squeezing real badly,
You can easily say his cocks got a real bad case of pox.
And you can pick it, you can scratch it, but if you ere can detach it,
You're better man than I am, Gunga Din.

HMS PEREGRINE, CIRCA 1956

The crew room for the ship's flight was an old WW2 wooden shack with a central coal-burning pillar-box stove to provide some much needed heat in winter.

Working on piston engines, frequently with petrol dripping down your hands and arms, was apt to get a bit chilly at times, especially out on the hard standing where the wind, rain and even snow, whipped around you.

One grew so cold at times it could take quite a few moments just to put down one spanner and pick up the next.

As there was seldom any coal for the stove in the crew room, Jack needed to use his nounce to find alternative combustible materials, such as wood, oily rags, yesterday's newspapers etc.

Whilst Pusser was somewhat reluctant to provide coal, they did provide plenty of rags for working on the aircraft engines and airframes. Jack found, by trial and error, oily rags were the best fuel for creating heat.

By judicious use of the flap of the ash clearance port at the bottom of the pillar-box shaped stove and the flap of the fuel re-filling port at the top to regulate airflow, with oily or aviation turbine fuel (AVTur) soaked rags quite a lot of heat could be generated, very quickly.

Once we had the stove going and set the flaps set to maximum efficiency, the stove-pipes chimney, or funnel as we referred to it, would start to glow red.

Starting at the cast iron fitting, where the chimney joined the stove base, someone chalked rings about two inches apart going up the pipe and marked each ring as a 'Temperature Gauge', indicated by the height the red glow caused by the stove would reach.

These rings were labelled thus.

Warm

Warmer

Nice

Hot

Red Hot

White Hot

Shit Hot

Clear the fuck out of the Crew room

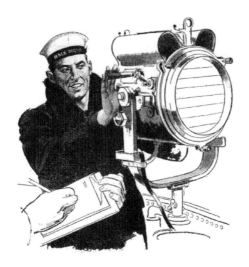

ONCE A SAILOR, ALWAYS A SAILOR

Anon

I remember standing on the foc'sle on a Morning watch weighing anchor with the smell of the North Wind whipping in from ahead and the taste of salt spray on my lips.

The feel of the ship beneath me, a living thing as her engines drive her through the sea.

The sounds of the Royal Navy, the piercing trill of the boatswain's call, the clang of the ships bell, the harsh squawk of the main broadcast Tannoy, and the strong language and laughter of sailors at work.

The warships, sleek destroyers, fussing frigates, plodding fleet auxiliaries, menacing submarines, purposeful mine hunters and steady solid carriers.

The proud names of the Royal Navy's capital ships, ARK ROYAL, EAGLE, LION and TIGER.

The descriptive names of destroyers, DARING, BIRMINGHAM, BATTLEAXE, CAVALIER, and frigates, ACTIVE, UNDAUNTED, VIGILANT to name just a few.

The military beat of the Royal Marine Band blaring on the upper deck as we entered harbour in Procedure Alpha.

The pipe "Liberty men fall in," and the spicy scent and sights of a foreign port.

Going ashore in No1 uniform to meet the ladies and visit the watering holes of these foreign ports.

My mates, men from all parts of the land, from city and country alike and all walks of life. I depended on them as they depended on me for professional competence, comradeship, trust and courage, in a word we were shipmates, a band of brothers.

A loud game of Uckers in the evening with my messmates.

My shipmate slinging my Mick (hammock) (or unzipping my pit) for me coming aboard after a run ashore, knowing I would do the same for him.

The surge of adventure in my heart when the calls of "Special Sea Duty men close up," or "Away sea boat's crew," were piped.

The absolute joy of hearing the call "Up Spirits" in anticipation of your daily tot of rum.

The sudden adrenalin rush when the "Action Stations" alarm blared, followed by the clamour of running feet on ladders and the resounding thump of watertight doors and hatches being shut as the ship transformed herself from a peaceful home to a deadly weapon of war, ready for anything.

The atmosphere of the ship in the darkness of night, the dim red glow of the night lights and the navigation lights.

Standing on the quarterdeck as "Lifebuoy Ghost" (*sentry*) watching the sparkling phosphorescence from the screws as they constantly pushed tons of water astern of the ship, carrying us to our next destination.

The "Watch on Deck" on a balmy tropical night in the South China sea watching the glorious sunset and flying fish gliding for amazing distances across the surface of the sea, with some landing inboard.

Drifting off to sleep in a hammock (or bunk), lulled by the myriad of noises large and small which told me my ship is alive and well and my shipmates were on watch, keeping me safe.

The aroma from the galley during the Morning Watch.
Cheesy, Hammy, Eggy, Train Smash, Shit on a Raft and Figgy Duff.

The wholesome taste of kai (very thick cocoa) during the middle watch on a cold, dark winters night.
The sound of the bow slicing through the mirror-calm of the sea and the frolicking of dolphins as they darted in and out of the bow wave.

Watching the ships wake disappearing towards the horizon, knowing it will be gone in a short time and being aware we were not the first, nor will we be the last, to leave our mark on the water.

The state-of-the-art equipment and the orange glow of radar screens, manned by young men in anti-flash gear using sound powered phones their grandfathers would recognise.

The infectious feeling of excitement as we returned home again, the hugs and kisses of welcome from sweethearts, family and friends.

The work was hard and dangerous, the going rough at times, the parting from loved ones painful but the robust Royal Navy comradeship, the *all for one and one for all* philosophy of the sea was ever-present.

The traditions of the Royal Navy, the men who made them and the heroism of the men who sailed in the ships of yesteryear.

Now I am home I still remember with fondness and respect, the sea in all its moods, from the shimmering mirror calm of the tropics to the storm-tossed waters of the North Atlantic.

I can still see the bright colours of the White Ensign snapping at the yardarm and the sound of hearty laughter whipped away by the squall.
I am ashore for good now and grow wistful about my Royal Navy days, days when I was young and a new adventure was waiting over every horizon.

Stamped on my brain is my Official Number and an anchor lays where my heart is.

Numbers will never be the same again: Uniforms: Number 1s 2s 3s 6s 8s 10s 10A's. Punishments: Number 9s, 14s.

Even as times change and young matelots take over from the old seadogs, some things will never change.

The old days were always harder.

The recruits always looked younger.

Official Numbers were always smaller.

The waves were always bigger.

The girls were as good looking in Pompey (Portsmouth) as they were in Guzz (Devonport).

Your last ship was always the best.

If I haven't been there, it doesn't exist - or we blew it off the map.

Only a sailor knows.

I was once a sailor, and I know.

I look back and realise it was not just a job, it was a way of life.
A life where shipmates were a family never to be forgotten.
I was part of the Royal Navy and the Royal Navy will always be part of me.

THEY SENT ME FOR...

A tin of Black Ham

A FANCY HAIRDO

An old three badge sludgemariner was sitting on a bench in the shopping centre, watching the world pass by when a youth with spiky purple, blue, green and yellow hair sat next to him.

The old guy couldn't take his eyes of the youth's coiffure.

The youth, becoming uncomfortable with the old hand staring at him said, rather rudely, *"What the fuck you looking at you old giffer, ain't you done anything a bit wild in your life?"*

Without taking a breath, the old hand said, *"Got pissed as a newt once, ended up shagging a parrot in Rio. So, I was just wondering if you were my son."*

NEW NAVAL DIRECTIVE REGARDING COMMUNICATION

"He's not trained to handle that equipment."

needs to be used instead of

"The thick cunts got his head up his fucking arse."

THE OLD GOAT

Leading goat Walter was H.M.S. Raleigh's mascot for around nine years, before being retired to Plymouth Zoo.

Walter's pen was about 20 yards from the canteen door.
While this was handy for the Galley cooks, who needed to supply Walter's food, it also meant the entire ship's company needed to pass Walter each scran time.

Walter was tethered to a stake, which was secured into the ground when he was not put away in his hut.

This stake had a large ring fixed into its top, through which a long rope, about fifteen yards long, ran attaching at the other end to Walter's collar.
This gave the old bastard plenty of freedom while keeping him from legging it.

Now, 'Jack', being right twats, found it highly amusing to annoy Walter, often by wriggling their arses, or 'mooning' the goat to get Walter to charge them.

As I have said previously, Walter was a cantankerous old bastard and it did not take much of this sort of encouragement to get Walters back up, so many times a day the goat tried to attack the annoying twats showing him their backsides.

What Jack found most amusing was the point when Walter came to the end of the rope, when it snapped him back almost breaking his neck or strangling him.

For some reason, Jack found this sudden halting of the goats charge hilarious and the crowd of goat teasers would piss themselves with laughter at the old bugger's misfortune. Especially as Walter never seemed to learn how long his tether was or when he should stop running.

Anyway, my boss at the time was a two ringer who, one evening, witnessed Walter's predicament.

Rather than trooping those he saw teasing Walter he ordered a new tethering rope.

The new rope was twenty-one yards long, six yards longer than before.

I'll leave it to your imagination to visualise what happened to the first arse wriggler who teased Walter following the rope exchange, except to say there was absolute panic milliseconds before the carnage.

I stood a little way back, in the company of our new two ringer and watched the whole show.

Absolutely hilarious.

THE VAN WITH THE SCRAN

Way back in the distant past (1966 to be exact), I was one of the watch-keepers in the Ground Radio Station on Camel Hill, adjacent to the main A303 road, about three miles from RNAS Yeovilton.

Because the radio station needed to be manned 24/7, our routine was 24 hours on and 24 hours off.

This meant we had our own fully equipped galley, which was victualed from the air station.

One night the Duty PO discovered we were running low of fresh scran, so he threw me the keys to a Bedford van we kept on-site, ordering me to drive to the few miles to Yeovilton and re-stock our supplies from the main galley.

He instructed me to get some steaks, joints of beef, and bacon and eggs for breakfasts.

I told the PO I couldn't drive, he said, "Don't fucking argue, just go and get our food."

I stood there open-mouthed, deciding whether he was joking or not, when he said, "For fuck sake, now's the time for you to learn... anyways, I'm getting my head down, so there is only you."

Well, there I was, in the pitch black, at three o'clock in the morning, crunching the gears and kangarooing down the A303 in this bloody van. However, I soon got the hang of things and, back then at that time of night there was very little traffic. The bobbies were all drinking mugs of tea as they sat around a cosy fire in their stations, so I felt reasonably safe from the long arms of the old bill.

After that trip, I volunteered to drive the van whenever I could, which gave me loads of practice before I eventually took my driving test.

Needless to say, I passed the first time.

Happy days.

FLEET AIR ARM

1960, SINGERS

A small group of us Airy-Fairies, off watch from Ark Royal in Singapore, went to the NAAFI club dance for a run ashore.

The killick of our mess, LAM(AE) 'Dolly', spotting an attractive young lady, went and politely asked if she would like to dance.

In a very loud voice, she replied, "Go to bed with you. NO Thank you."

I'd never seen Dolly blush before, he came back to his Tiger beer and sat down, disgruntled, even a tad embarrassed.

A few moments later the young lady came to our table and quietly said to Dolly, "I'm sorry about that, but I'm studying psychology and wanted to see your reaction."

Dolly, at the top of his best parade ground voice, replied...

"Fifty Quid, you can fuck off."

We pissed ourselves laughing.

I think the girl learnt something important about applied psychology that day... when it's applied to sailors that is.

I woke up this morning at 8:00hrs.

I could smell something was wrong.

When I got downstairs, I found the wife face down on the kitchen floor.

She was not breathing, I panicked.

I didn't know what to do.

Then I remembered... McDonald's serves breakfast until 11:30.

Panic over

SECRET TUNNELS

AND BACON BUTTIES

Admiralty 1956/57 (ish)

Often, towards the end of a night-watch, we would be assigned to be the 'Incinerator party' and needed to go along one of the tunnels under Horseguards.

It was pretty spooky, requiring us to be issued with protection... in the form of military-grade broom handles. As it is, the worst thing we ever encountered were those big fuck off bastard rats. Thankfully, they were more frightened of us than we were of them... or so we told one another.

Now, these secret tunnels are a couple of hundred feet under the citadel. There was quite a maze of them, many with heavy, locked and barred doors. These, we were informed, led to, or gave alternative access to important locations such as No10 Downing Street, Buckingham Palace and the War Registry.

Others led to certain tube stations, some of which are not on any map or part of a regular line and were last seriously used during World War II, before being closed.

Often, during a night-watch, we would explore the tunnels even though we found access to anywhere interesting was usually barred or would necessitate climbing up or down iron ladders which disappeared into the darkness of mysterious shafts.

Once, in the early hours, three of us plucked up the courage to climb one of these shafts. It went on for far longer than we anticipated but, at the top was a small landing, a platform with a large metal door. It was like something from a James Bond film.

I pushed the door, not expecting it to move. To our astonishment, it swung open to reveal a grand office, all thick carpet, mahogany bookcases and heavy wooden desk. We crept around the room, almost tiptoeing as not to disturb anything when the door through which we entered swung shut.

We could not fathom out how to open the door from inside the room. The only way we could see to get out was through the main door, which was on the opposite side of the room.

Cracking the door open we peered out. There was a long, well-lit corridor that seemed to stretch away to infinity. This was the only option we had, so I took a deep breath and led us brazenly from the room, striding along the corridor as if we were supposed to be there and, what's more, knew where in the heck we were going.

After several paces, the shout came "Halt, who goes there". Yep, I shit you not, that was what they called out to us. Crapping our collective shitniks, we turned around to be faced by two RAF Regiment crabfats pointing a pair of the new L1A1 SLR rifles at our chests.

Luckily, the poor chaps swallowed the feed of shit we gave them about being left behind and needing to get back before the end of watch. Kindly they showed (*escorted*) us to the exit, which turned out to be the Air Ministry.

Now, the Air Ministry is, as you may know, on the opposite side of Horseguard's Parade to Whitehall Wireless, (*where we were meant to still be on duty.*) It was amazing to find out how far we travelled underground.

It was an adventure I shall never forget and one which was nicely rounded off because, as we returned the Admiralty, the smell of eggy baccy butties being knocked up for our breakfast by the watch AB wafted through the air.

I will always associate that smell with the Mob.

Class.

SIGN IN A BANGKOK TEMPLE, THAILAND

"It is forbidden to enter a woman, even a foreigner if dressed as a man."

THE SAILOR'S TEN COMMANDMENTS

1. Thou shalt not scrounge, neither shalt thou swing the lead, lest they resting place be the deep waters upon which thou sail.

2. Thou shalt not take the name of the Petty Officer in vain or thou shalt have thy name inscribed upon the books of the Commander and thou shalt embark on a course of Chokey.

3. Honour the Master at Arms and the R.P.O. all the days of thy service that they credit you thy credits be numbered even as the fishes below thee.

4. Thou shalt not fill thyself to overflowing with beer, or by Royal Warrant thou shalt lose much of thy pay, and the Master at Arms shalt number thee amongst his flock, for it is written that he who drinketh to excess shall bash the square.

5. Six days shalt thou labour and on the seventh thou shalt do twice as much.

6. If it comes to pass that thy zeal and the sweat of thy brow cause mention of thee in the wardroom, and thou art elevated to the dizzy heights of AB, Lo, thou shalt present thy humble body at thy canteen and shall crave thy messmates accept sippers of thy ale all around.

7. Thou shalt not take unto thyself they comrade's kit, neither shalt thou borrow when the owner thereof is not present or thy sins will be visited upon thee by the quickness of the hand that blacketh the eye.

8. Thou shalt not fritter away they worldly goods by playing Crown and Anchor lest the avenging voice of the R.P.O. be heard to say, "Render unto me the names and let thy money remain where it lieth".

9. Though shalt not kill if the Petty Officer grieveth thee. Thou shalt not smite him, neither shalt thou sling him over the side. Thou shalt go unto the top man and crave audience with him and set forth they grievance with much wailing and gnashing of teeth. He shall open his mouth and words of wisdom shall flow forth, next time it shall be even twice as bad.

10. And when it shall come to pass that thou has finished thy time, thou shalt embark upon the waters and journey thereon until thou reachest thy home port. There thou shalt take thyself strange garments and shall be known as a civvy in the land, and thou shalt study the dole and the drawing thereof, and so for many years thou shalt take it easy and rest from thy labours.

NEW NAVAL DIRECTIVE REGARDING COMMUNICATION

The words,
"Really?" or "Honestly?"

posed as a question should be used
instead of,

"Well fuck me backwards, knobhead."

RADIO REVELATION

One from an Aussie matelot who swears this is a Gen dit.

FOX FM, Sydney. Morning radio show.

Imagine... you're sitting in your car on the way in, listening to 'Mate Match', a game where the DJ calls someone and askes three personal questions.

The DJ then calls the person's partner/wife/girl-boyfriend and asks the same three questions. If the partner gives the same answers, they both win a prize.

This is what happened one morning...

DJ: 'Hey! This is Ed on FOX-FM. Have you ever heard of 'Mate Match?''

Contestant: (laughing). 'Yes, I have.'

DJ: 'Great. Then you know we're giving away a trip to the Gold Coast if you win.

DJ: 'What is your name? First only please.'

Contestant: 'Brian.'

DJ: 'Brian, are you married or what?'

Brian: (*laughing nervously),* 'Yes, I am married.'

DJ: 'Thank you. Now, what is your wife's name? First only please.'

Brian: 'Sara.'

DJ: 'Is Sara at work, Brian?'

Brian: 'She is gonna kill me.'

DJ: 'Stay with me here, Brian. Is she at work?'

Brian: (*laughing*), 'Yes, she's at work.'

DJ: 'Okay, the first question - when was the last time you had sex?'

Brian: 'About 8 o'clock this morning.'

DJ: 'Atta boy, Brian.'

Brian: (*laughing sheepishly*), 'Well...'

DJ: 'Question 2 - How long did it last?'

Brian: 'About 10 minutes.'

DJ: 'Wow! You really want that trip, huh? No one would ever have said that if a trip wasn't at stake.'

Brian: 'Yeah, that trip sure would be nice.'

DJ: 'Okay. Final question. Where did you have sex at 8 o'clock this morning?

Brian: (*laughing hard*) 'I, ummm, I, well...'

DJ: 'This sounds good, Brian. Where was it at?'

Brian: 'Not that it was all that great, but her mum is staying with us for a couple of weeks...'

DJ: 'Uh-huh...'

Brian: '...and the Mother-In-Law was in the shower at the time.'

DJ: 'Atta boy, Brian.'

Brian: 'On the kitchen table.'

DJ: 'Not that great? That is more adventure than the previous hundred times I've done it.

Okay, folks, I will put Brian on hold, get his wife's work number and call her up.

You listen to this.'

[3 minutes of commercials.]

DJ: 'Okay audience; let's call Sarah, shall we?' (*Touch tones.....ringing....*)

Clerk: 'Kinkos.'

DJ: 'Hey, is Sarah around there somewhere?'

Clerk: 'This is she.'

DJ: 'Sarah, this is Ed with FOX-FM. We are live on the air right now and I've been talking with Brian for a couple of hours now.'

Sarah: (*laughing*) 'A couple of hours?'

DJ: 'Well, a while now. He is on the line with us. Brian knows not to give any answers away or you'll lose. Sooooooo... do you know the rules of 'Mate Match'?'

Sarah: 'No.'

DJ: 'Good!'

Brian: (*laughing*)

Sarah: (*laughing*) 'Brian, what the hell are you up to?'

Brian: (*laughing*) 'Just answer his questions honestly, okay? Be completely honest.'

DJ: 'Yeah yeah yeah. Sure. Now, I will ask you 3 questions, Sarah. If your answers match Brian's answers, then both of you will be off to the Gold Coast for 5 days on us.

Sarah: (*laughing*) 'Yes.'

DJ: 'Alright. When did you last have sex, Sarah?'

Sarah: 'Oh God, Brian.....uh, this morning before Brian went to work.'

DJ: 'What time?'

Sarah: 'Around 8 this morning.'

DJ: 'Very good. Next question. How long did it last?'

Sarah: '12, 15 minutes maybe.'

DJ: 'Hmmmm. That's close enough. I am sure she is trying to protect his manhood. We've got one last question, Sarah. You are one question away from a trip to the Gold Coast. Are you ready?'

Sarah: (*laughing*) 'Yes.'

DJ: 'Where did you have it?'

Sarah: 'OH MY GOD, BRIAN. You didn't tell them that did you?'

Brian: 'Just tell him, honey.'

DJ: 'What is bothering you so much, Sarah?'

Sarah: 'Well...'

DJ: Come on Sarah... where did you have it?

Sarah: 'Up the arse...'

The station had to call an ambulance for the DJ, they thought he was going to have a heart attack because he could not stop laughing.

Apparently, there was also an unusually high call out of the Sydney Police just after this conversation for minor traffic collisions.

.

GEN PIPE

We had a sprog blurt out over the Tannoy, during a refit,

'Dockyard Rigger Mortice - to the Sickbay'·

THE LEGEND OF PALAU TIOMAN

You can't beat a Banyan

Pulau Tioman is the location used in the film South Pacific. Watch it and you will see a large waterfall while they are singing "I'm gonna wash that man right outta my hair."

No doubt it has changed in the ensuing years, but back in 1965, it was pretty much as you see in the film.

The lads were playing football on the beach, well, an improvised version using a coconut as the ball. The pain of broken toes and what they call metatarsals nowadays, the things we used to call feet, were not felt until the following day due to the aesthetic qualities of several cans of brew.

Some who did not experience sporting injuries suffered a pain of another kind when stepping on sea-urchins. Those nasty little spines, which are formed like a stack of vending cups, take several years to work themselves from the body, which is why it was advisable to wear gutties or sandals.

So, there we are, booting a coconut along the beach when out of the undergrowth comes a moped. Not just rumbling along but flying through the air like Steve McQueen in the Great Escape.

The bike comes to a standstill and J**** is sat on it, grinning like the proverbial Cheshire cat, although that may be the proverbial Cheshire housewife nowadays, anyway...

Someone climbed on the bike behind J**** and he revved the bugger until it screamed. Once on, the passenger, (*I think it was JP?)* lifted his legs and put them on the footpegs.

We stood staring, expecting the bike to shoot up the beach spaying a cloud of sand and shite in its wake but the whole thing just keeled over to starboard.

It seems soft sand and narrow tyres are not ideal companions.

JP was dripping about his knee, J**** was pissing his arse off, as were the rest of us. I don't recall much after that, except for some more beers and a barbecue.

I have no idea where the moped came from or where it went but I do know that legend has it, if you dig down far enough into the sand on that beach you can still find tins of 'Tiger Beer' Jack buried to keep cold during the banyan and then forgot where he put the buggers.

Happy Daze, wot.

THE CO's FLOWERS

I was on a leadership course at Royal Arthur back in the '90s.

Chief GI 'Legs' Diamond was a legendary figure on the base, partly because of his, umm, often eccentric behaviour.

Once he was passing the CO's garden and stood for a while scowling at the CO's wife while she was planting flowers in the garden.

Feeling somewhat uncomfortable with the chief's attention she said, in an attempt to break the ice, "Good morning, Chief."

The chief answered politely, "Good morning ma'am" but continued to scowl.

"May I help you, Chief?" the CO's wife asked, now becoming irritated.

The chief replied, "Them flowers is all out of line ma'am."

He then marched away.

THEY SENT ME FOR,

A left-handed box spanner.

ADEN, KRAYTER AND A LOAD OF ARMY BOLLOCKS

On an aircraft carrier, I'll not say which, anchored in Aden harbour. The other ships at anchor or tied up to the buoys. The fleet is scheduled to be in harbour for 5 days.

Bum boats are taking sailors ashore, while a couple of harbour launches are doing a run around the fleet.

'*We*' get ashore, along with hundreds of other sailors from the fleet, all landing on the jetty at around the same time. Most were stood around, huddled together in their little sore parties, smoking and discussing where to go.

And that was the question, where to go?

My group, I think there must have been ten of us, decided to get taxies into the local town. Aden is not, or at least was not, the type of place to be wandering around alone, or even in a pair. Staying together in larger groups was the safest way. The place was one of the arseholes of the world, one with crabs and shitty stains too.

Arriving in the town we found a bar and was made welcome by the owner. The chap's eyes gleaming, giving us the toothy broad smile as he weighed up how much money he could fleece us for.

Half a beer down and the Army patrol arrives. They unceremoniously kick us out. They said this bar is not one 'officially recognised' by the Red Caps.

This was despite the protestations by the landlord, who was unhappy watching his potential profit being given the old heave-ho.

The second bar we found was busier and, to be honest, quite a lot smarter in comparison.

We got ourselves some cold beers, settled into some comfy chairs and were happily nattering away when an Army Officer, accompanied by a few of his cronies, came into the bar. As soon as he saw us he asks for us to be immediately ejected. It seems this was an officer's bar and we, being lowly Jack the lads, were clearly unwelcome.

Bar number three was packed to the gunnels with matelots of all nationalities. It was dirty, noisy and looked like the perfect place where we could neck a few bevvies without being asked to leave by the military Police or the knobsworth-jobsworth army officer corps.

But it was not to be.

Just our luck, the moment we arrived a massive multi-national fight broke out. Within a moment the Army patrol arrived and clears the place out. Every single body military bod ejected into the street. The bar was closed to all servicemen for the rest of the night.

And so, it continued.

At this point, we had been ashore for about three hours and not yet got a decent drink inside us.

We were excluded from the Army canteen. We were 'discouraged' from visiting any service base, not allowed onto any of the family beaches, and henceforth the beach bars and cafes along those beaches. Everywhere we tried, either for a whet, a bit of scran, or simply a cold goffers, was 'out-of-bounds'.

This is when one of the old hands, a three badger who had been there and done that (twice), decided our only option for any form of entertainment or relaxation would be to get a cab to Crater City. Actually, it was a large town simply called Krayter, but somehow Crater city sounded better and that, even now, is how I think of the place. (*By the way, Krater's name nowadays is Seera.*)

Most taxi drivers refused to take us, telling us there was too much fighting in Crater City. By now we were getting desperate, and after what we had witnessed in the bars here, seeing another fight or two was not going to dissuade us from getting a beer or two down our necks, anywhere.

For once, luck was on our side, a bus or coach or sharrabang, whatever you like to call it, picked us up and we were off to Crater City for a beer and maybe some titty? Oh, our little group had grown to around fifteen or so and we were all gasping for a long cold one to wash the dust from our gullets.

After a rough ride along dirt roads, we arrived in the godforsaken city of 'Krayter'. Unperturbed, we all piled off the bus and straight into a large bar, full of booze and women. It was like heaven had opened its doors after what we had been through.

The night had definitely picked up and we got the old three badge OD an extra bottle or two for his idea of getting away from the shitehole that was Aden city.

Much later we heard a lot of noise outside and watched the owner closed and bolt the doors. "Yeah," we said, "we've got a lock-in", giggling like schoolboys.

The noise slowly got louder as the ruckus got nearer. Soon it was coming from directly outside the bar. We could not only hear the shouting, but there was a hell of a lot of gunfire accompanying it.

Beginning to shit me nicks and being half-drunk, I tried to leave, but was pulled were pulled back by a large Arab chap with a rifle. He said we needed to stay inside, then we would not, most probably, be harmed.

There was not much more we could do, so we carried on drinking, even if we were in a little more of a sombre mood.

About two hours later, it was 2330, the coach-bus thingy turned up and we were herded aboard, under the protection of the big Arab, his friends and their rifles. The bus took us back to Aden Dockside.

It was an uneventful journey.

However, many of us younger ones were on Cinderella leave so, by the time we staggered onto the dockside it was way beyond that time, which was an issue... not only for us but the hundreds of other sailors waiting for the non-existent liberty boats to ferry them back to their ships.

The matelots on the wharf were from many nations and most were as pissed as newts. The waiting saw tempers fray as impatience grew. This led to frequent small fights breaking out, sending a further ripple of discontent along the dockside, creating more isolated scuffles and more ripples.

The shore patrols were mainly Army Redcaps, with some la-de-dah officer in charge who was attempting to order hundreds of drunken sailors to fall-in and report in an orderly manner, so he could press charges against them for being outside curfew, (After 2359).

Curfew... what curfew? We were not informed of any curfew.

What the officer did not take into consideration was most of the seafarers along the dockside could not speak or understand a single word of English.

Not getting much joy from shouting, the Redcap officer ordered his Landcovers to herd the bodies into one area of the quayside. This was when an argument, resulting in a Redcap punching a young sailor, from one of our frigates, right on his nose.

That was the last straw. The Navies rose, all of them, man and boy from every country represented on that dock. The whole area was now one big boxing match, Navy(s) against Army and RAF patrols.

Without any exaggeration, there were easily 2500 pissed off sailors, returning from a shit run ashore, being constantly hassled by the brown jobs for no true reason, when all they wanted is to get back on board and get their heads down.

No lies, even the Sailors on shore patrol took off their webbing and joined in the melee, which, by now, involved some of the Army vehicles being launched into the oggin.

We were informed the following day that the sinking of fifteen Army vehicles along with a count of approximately 200 injuries needing medical treatment, mostly belonging to the Redcaps and RAF police was not conducive with Royal Navy standards.

Therefore, the Admiral informed us, all shore leave in Aden City and Krayter would be immediately suspended. His paperwork complete and telex sent to London the Admiral informed the Army and RAF he had taken all appropriate actions.

The fleet sailed the following morning.

Not a single Royal Navy ship was scheduled to return during this commission.

This left a very pissed off Army to recover their vehicles.

Krayter was declared out-of-bounds to all servicemen, officially due to terrorist activities. Although not a single sailor was hurt at the time.

Aden was not a good run ashore and, as far as I understand, still not a place I would recommend anyone visiting, in any capacity.

LEUCHARS AND THE SARNIE INCIDENT

I was on 892 squadron. We were at Leuchars which, by the way, closed in 2011 as part of the defence cuts.
Anyways, on wiv me dit...

Now, we used to get aircraft coming into Leuchars for various reasons, most it seemed random, but who the fuck knows? 'cause no one told us 'owt.

We just did what we got told and then got pissed and then slept. This particular night we were nearly finished when I got a phone call.

Two planes had landed but were only refuelling as they were heading on southward. The piolets asked for some sarnies sent over to keep 'um going.

This being an RAF base, we had one of their flight sergeants in charge, a bloke called Joe if I remember rightly.

This Joe says to me, "For Fucks sake, it always happens just when I want to get me head down." He carries on, "Macca, (*that's me*), make those sarnies up and send that prat Chris out to deliver them. Then get your head down, I'm off for me own zed's right now." And off he trotted.

I did a 'proper job' with those butties, cut the crusts off, sliced 'um into dainty(ish) triangles, packed everything neatly into tiddly brown bags.

I then shouts for Chris. "I'm off mate,"

I says, handing him the bags. "Take them over the airfield for us, mate, I need to get some shut-eye." With that I'm off, scuttling away for a swift bevy in the NAFFI before it closes, then I'm crawling into me pit.

Comes in the next morning and Sergeant Joe is going ape-shite. Seems Chris delivered two bags of crusts to the waiting planes. Fucked if I know how that happened.

Sadly, Joe has crossed the bar now, or whatever it is that Crab Fats do.

THE CHEESEBOARD

Pompey Dockyard circa 1988.

HMS Birmingham.

My first ever solo duty.

I had the responsibility for ensuring the Officers Mess evening meal ran smoothly, with expert professional service.

No worries. Soup starter, two choices of main and a cheeseboard replacing the standard dessert.

Piece of piss, methinks.

As a sprog, I was up for the challenge of proving I was competent to carry out my duties alone.

I set about my preparation, soon it was time to organising the cheeseboard. I opened the fridge and blow me down, no frigging cheese.

Some twat was winding me up.

Time was ticking away and I admit my arsehole gave a little bit of a twitch.

I decided to go to the main galley below and see the Duty Chef who was now busy slaving away feeding the remainder of the Ships Company.

Even so, as he was a good lad and told me to "help myself," indicating with a jerk of his thumb as he said, "there's some over there."

I wandered over to the far side of the galley and looked under the greaseproof paper on the beach I did think this was not the best-looking cheese I have ever seen. It looked a bit dry and crinkly but it was cut into cubes as you see with pineapple and cocktail sticks.

I didn't want to whinge to the cook, who was running around like a headless chicken feeding the troops. So, I didn't ask him if I could rummage around in the main fridge, besides, time was pushing on and I needed to get back to the pigsty.

I would just have to get creative with what I had.

Back in the wardroom, I built a terrific pyramid, each little cube stacked on another, Jenga style. I then scattered a bit of green, nuts and other such shite around the edge of the silver platter. All in all, I was rather pleased with my efforts seeing the poor choice of ingredients I had to work with.

The evening meal was going without a hitch; starter cleared away, the main course done. Wine flowing, the Officers seemed content.

Then it was time for my artistic masterpiece of a cheeseboard.

I placed the plates, butter and biscuits on the table, steadily carried the cheese pyramid over and set it gently in the centre for all to admire.

I was a happy bunny... until...

All conversation came to an abrupt halt and a silence came over the table, wine held suspended mid-air as the XO asked me...

"What the hell is this?"

"It's a cheeseboard, Sir," I answered nervously. I knew it looked a bit wrinkly, but surely it was not that bad?

Nervously I continued to babble, "I couldn't get any cheese from the fridge, Sir. The main galley cook was busy serving the ship's company. It's the only cheese I could find, Sir."

To be honest I didn't know what the problem was but was now shitting my nicks when the entire table burst out laughing.

I was now even more filled with fear and dread as I had no idea what caused the outburst. Why were they all in fits of hysterical laughter?

I was clueless.

The XO spoke again "Lad," he said, "you have excelled. In all my years in the Royal Navy, I have never finished a meal in this way."

"What is it, Sir?" I asked, shaking.

"This cheeseboard, lad. It is the strangest cheeseboard I have ever had the delight to experience."

"Sorry Sir, but as I said, I couldn't find any other cheese. What's wrong with it, Sir?"

"It's not cheese, lad," he replied, "it's swede. Bloody raw swede."

ALONGSIDE LEGENDS

Anymouse?

We've served alongside legends, some still famous in the fleet,

whose exploits on a run ashore were simply hard to beat.

With Jocks and Geordies and the rest from all around this land,

we've sailed and drunk and ate with them. This buccaneering band.

With quiet guys who don't say much and those who like to fight,

We've shared some sunny tropic days and stormy seas at night.

We did our bit for Britain, our duty to the Queen,

We've done our part as best we could by ship and submarine.

With those who flew our aircraft and by many other means,

Like those seaborne raiders, Her Majesty's Marines.

We did our thing around the world, our pride on show for all,

Royal Navy Men and Women, all answering the call.

No longer is our naval fleet a force of many ships.

We used to show our British flag on long and splendid trips.

No longer then is this the case, our world has gone through change.

A sadder, more violent place, dangerous and strange.

The sailor's job is always there and always will be too,

For even with less fighting ships, those ships still need a crew.

So whatever era that you served, from days of steam to now,

Be proud of what you all once did, salute and take a bow.

There's one thing that bonds us matelots, that gels us all together,

when facing foreign dangers or battling stormy weather.

When struggling through FOST workups, or marching to the band

On never-ending cleaning teams with stroppy Leading Hands.

On sun-kissed, beery barbecues, cold refit ships at night,

Those lonely months away from home, high seas that cause us fright,

Shipmates laughing in the mess, playing messdeck games.

A call to action, fire or flood, men lost... we know their names.

It's the knowledge deep within our hearts, we have each other's back.

We're all of one great company, us sailors, known as 'Jack'.

*"I've had a wonderful day . . .
never felt nastier!"*

AUTHORS NOTE
regarding the following pages

While compiling **Jacks Dits 2,** I came across many short, yet hilarious dits which deserve airing in this book.

It is those short dits that fill the following pages.

Enjoy the madness.

GENUINE SIGN

Doctor's office, Rome:

"Specialist in women and other diseases".

PRACTISING FOR THE JUBILEE

This was 1977, Silver Jubilee year.

For some unknown reason, they had a Yank in charge of the I.S platoon.

Typical looking Yank, shite haircut, thick horn-rimmed specs. Looked like a total dickhead.

We were on the parade ground going through the early stages of the square bashing we would end up performing on the day.

At a certain point, the Yank shouted, "Bugler, sound the call."

The bugler was a rough as fuck AB, from the Aussie Navy. He replied, "I don't have a bugle yet, Sir, they've not issued one to me."

The Yank ignored the Aussie, insisting he obeys the order and 'sound the frigging horn'.

The poor Aussie sod had to give in and began shouting, "Ta da da daa".

The Yank then seemed happy... until we could not keep ourselves together and fell about laughing our head off.

The whole day turned into ratshite after that.

Fucking fantastic.

Happy days.

DIM REGULATOR

HMS Pembroke, Chatham

I joined East Camp from Ganges at the end of August '75, D151, as an ACK.

My first order was to go to the Guardroom, all the way from East Camp and get a 'Dim Regulator'.

I was told to go 'on the double' and not to hang around because they were waiting for one.

So, as good as gold, off I trot.

If you have been to Pembroke you'll know the main drag is almost straight for a good old distance, which makes it seem even further than the fair old jaunt it is from the huts to the other end of the base, the Guardroom being near the main gate.

Like a good little sprog, I doubled the entire distance, not sloping off as I learnt to do later whenever the opportunity arose.

By the time I got there, I was shagged out.

I don't think the RPO was that impressed with my request for a dim regulator, although he let me sit in a cell while I regained my breath.

A POCKET BURGER

We are alongside in Pompey.

Every bugger is going ashore on the lash, except me. I was duty sparker.

They all did the usual shit, shave, shower and shampoo bit, before prancing around the mess Ironing shirts, wafting foo-foo dust, spraying clouds of deodorant shite and combing their receding hairlines.

The mess ending up smelling like the bottom of a whore's handbag, or just the bottom of a whore... not that I know what either smells like, of course.

On their way out of the mess, somebody asked if I wanted big eats bringing back.

I said, "If it's not too late, I'll have a cheeseburger."

Then they all buggered off ashore, the mess suddenly silent.

Well, not much was doing, so, I thought I'll get me head down early.

I was having a lovely kip when I heard a "pssssstt" in my ear'ole.

I thought I was dreaming, but it came again. "psssssssssstttt", longer and louder this time.

I lifted my head from the pillow and squinted at my Seiko. It was 04.15hrs.

In the dull light, I could just make out a figure stood beside me pit. He was rocking about a bit as he struggled to stay upright. He was as hammered as a dockyard rat.

"Now, mate," he says, waving an unsteady finger in my face.

I watched as he started struggling to pull something from his pocket. At one point, losing his balance and staggering forward, head-butting the base of the top pit. Then, with a grunt of triumph, he produced a paper-wrapped bundle and tossed it to me.

"There you go, fuck face," he said, lurching away as if we were in a force nine.

I picked the paper package off the counterpane, and read the faint yellow writing, it said, 'Cheeseburger'.

As you can imagine, it was cold. The cheese and scraping of tomato sauce congealed. It was not in the best of shape either and not just from being rammed into my oppo's pocket. I am certain its odd shape was due to being trodden on, possibly as he staggered from the taxi.

Even so, I gratefully ate it.

Knowing my oppo was completely off his tits, had virtually lost control of his limbs, but he hadn't forgotten his mate is the sort of thing I miss about the mob.

You don't get that connection in civvy street, not even from your bestie.

GEN NOTICE

While in Pompey Dock

Scouts are saving aluminium cans, bottles, and other items to be recycled.

Proceeds will be used to cripple children.

BREWING UP... OR NOT

I complained about making a brew whilst on the Berwick (F115).

The Killick sparker said, "Don't worry, then."

He sent someone else to make a pot of NATO Standard for the watch.

Later that day he called me, asking me to help him at the shredder, as I got near to where he was standing, someone wielded a metal teapot at me.

It flew around the corner, hitting me smack in the gish.

"Now," said the Killick, "go and make a fucking brew."

I took the pot and went down the main drag to the Jackson. Blood was still pouring from my nose and I got another bollicking from the Joss for making a mess in the flats.

He never asked how, or why I was bleeding. Just told me to clean it up.

Strangely, I never dripped about brewing up again.

MEMORIES OF PINKYS, WAN CHAI, HONG KONG

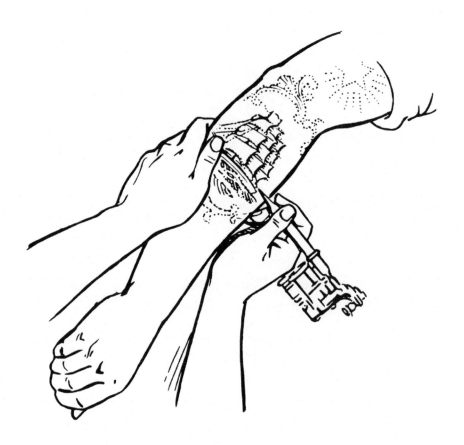

FLIGHT OF THE BUDGIES

It was the first Gulf conflict, the one where Saddam Hussein invaded Kuwait in 1990. Only by the time of this dit, it was already 1991.

I was the CRS on Manchester on the way out. We stopped off at Gibraltar.

For some reason, the schoolchildren gave the ship some Budgies. It was thought by the kids they would work like Canaries down a mine and give us some warning of gas or chemical attack.

Whatever the reason, each department was issued one budgie each.

I think the lads liked them, apart from the cleaning up their shit, of course.

Funnily enough, they never crapped on anyone, except the pilot when he came to read the signals.

When we got back at Gibraltar we needed to return the birds to the school.

It was to be a formal ceremony where we, the ship's company, were to give a resounding cheer, as in a loud, 'Hip, Hip, Hooray', as we handed over each bird in turn, thus honouring their 'service' during our tour in the warzone.

Unfortunately, someone didn't shut the cage properly and the little buggers flew away when the door to the MCO was left open.

The ceremony never took place and the school lost their budgerigars.

Not the best PR exercise conducted by the ship.

But hey, a bird on the wing and all that?... No.

Never mind.

HMS HERON

The admin office MACCO at HMS Heron, when a CPO walked in to join the ships company.

He spy's the two MAA's sat at the front desks and, straight out, he says, "Right then, which one of you can read and which one can write then?"

The two Jossmen look at each other, then at the Chief and one says, "I think you need to go outside and come back in again."

The Chief leaves. You can see him, through the windows, wandering around puffing away on a blueliner.

Fifteen minutes later the Chief comes back into the office, he says, " Was that long enough for you to work out which one of you can read and which one can write?"

Unable to control ourselves, the entire office burst out laughing.

Both the Joss's screamed at the CPO, at the top of their voices, "Get out."

I can't remember the CPO's name, but he deffo set the mood for the day.

Fucking BZ

PRESENT ARMS

GI. Parade ground.

"Now you lot," he says.

We thought, what a nice guy.

"We are going to do the 'Present Arms'. I will demonstrate. You will watch and listen and then you'll do it... perfectly, first time and with no mistakes... have you got me?"

We glanced at each other as we answered, "Yes, Chief." in unison, knowing we would all fuck it up anyway.

He continued, seemingly unphased by our blank-faced, incomprehensible stares.

"Left arm straight down, full extension," right comes smartly across the chest, grabbing the furniture, here. "Bring the rifle upright to your front, turning it and slam the furniture... and I want it slapped hard, one crack, hit as hard as you like, you will not break it."

He slapped the rifle smartly, one resounding crack... the rifle disintegrated in his hands.

Without a break in his spiel, he says, "That just shows you how hard I hit the fucker."

This event happened about sixty years ago.

It has always lived with me.

SHIT JOB

Only submariners will understand.

We were in Stavanger, Norway.

Upholder.

I had to blow shit overboard to a tanker.

At this time, the jetty was awash with fanny as the locals came to gawk at the boat.

I was getting bored; it was taking much too long to vent.

So, to hurry the process along I pressed the shitter valve.

The bugger backfired and blew shit all over me. Leaving a 'clean' silhouette of me masked out on the bulkhead.

Went back on the casing the trot sentry pissed himself laughing at me.

He said it looked like I had a dose of the brown measles.

Lesson learned; patience is a virtue.

A FUCKING FLAPPY THING

I think we were in the Indian Ocean, Bay of Bengal(ish), heading for Singers, but my mind is so fucked nowadays who knows? except to say we were out on the oggin and it was bloody hot.

Aywayhow, Tiger was an old girl and the Punkah louvre was blowing out little more ventilation than your oppos warm farts do during the night. So, as with many an old ship, we opened the scuttles and stuck out the wind scoops.

We had two such scuttles, one near the rear of the mess, the other in the mess square.

To wander off subject for a moment...

The scuttle in the mess square bulkhead was a bit of a, um, a liability really. You see, the only place we could put the television was just in front of it, on the back of the bench seating. This was, for you younger readers, when televisions were a little more substantial than the wafer-thin, all singing, all dancing, electro gizmos of today.

Many times, a goffer found its way through the scuttle and into the back of the TV set. Unfortunately, this was often when the evenings' film was showing and just when the man with the wooden eyeball was about to get his revenge/the girl/die, whatever.

Most times the 'tele' dried out over a couple of days. Once or twice it was washed off the side, until someone had the bright idea of securing it in place with bolts. The times it was completely fucked the mess funds or beer funds subsidised a replacement.

Now, back to the dit...

Picture this if you will, an average evening in the mess. All sat around in the square, Chase the Pisser being played one side, Risk the other, books being read, beer being drunk, jokes told, black cats bragged, Blue liners smoked, Tannoy playing a 'tune' form a wannabe DJ cookie boy in the SRE compartment far below.

Then, one of those goffers comes splashing up the ship's side, oggin caught in the wind scoop and directed into the mess. Big splash, soaking some, others laughing at them.

Then some big 'Fucking Flappy thing' lands smack bang in the middle of the Risk board sending all those little coloured counters flaying all over.

Every one of those hairy arsed, Beer swilling, John Collins drinking, Pinky Tattooed, Womanising matelots shits their kegs, jumping on the bunks, legging it away and scrambling for cover like a bunch of slack tarts, and all because one 'Fucking Flappy Thing', otherwise known as a Flying fish, landed on the mess square table.

Laugh my fucking bollocks off.

THE MICROWAVE FIASCO OF '79.

We went down to 28 people onboard and living out of Nelson. Tiger was dead waiting to be taken to the trots. We had enough power for some lighting and 3 sockets, one of which we had a microwave (*fairly new tech then*).

Anyway, we were doing 48 on 48 off, our meals sent over from Nelson ready-made up and on plates. All we needed to do was re-heat them. We put four plates in at a time, with ally rings keeping them separate, day two and the microwave started to crackle, sparks flying and smoke.

That was number one knackered.

They sent another, again after a couple of days it went bang. Oops, number two gizmo knackered.

There was hell on.

These microwaves were simple to operate. They had only a timer dial and a start button.

The next day a two-ringer comes aboard and gives us a dressing down for breaking 'his' microwaves.

"It's simple," he says, "watch."

The Lieutenant puts the meals in, turns the timer then presses the start button.

"There, simple," he repeats, just as the thing starts to crackle and sending sparks and smoke into the air.

New tech number three buggered.

We couldn't stop laughing.

He was bloody fuming.

The outcome was, many of the meals were being sent to us on wardroom plates, ones which had gold rings painted around their edges and could not be used in microwaves.

I am still laughing as I think about that poor Subbie's face.

He was so convinced it was us fucking up.

THE MISSING BOX

In '63 we went to Antwerp; I went ashore with the gash bin and shot across the road for a quick pint, still in my chefs' whites.

When I came back aboard my mate AK said I should do the same again but with him this time as he was the Killick.

So, we gather another load of gash and down the gangplank we go.

This time, AK has a box under his arm and, when we get to ditch the gash he pulls out his civvies and gets changed.

As planned, we trot over to the pub, me in whites, AK in his civvies. A couple of swift(ish) pints and back we go.

The disaster is, the box with AK's whites is gone. He starts panicking and kicking off, swearing and threatening to kill 'some bastard' when he gets his hands on them, not knowing who moved his box.

The only option was for him to walk onboard and brazen it out.

It did not work. The OOD had heard AK shouting and listened in.

I got seven days in the cells while AK lost his hook.

Of course, I've never done anything like that again, honest.

THE BIG BANG

I was one of the fish-heads stationed at RNAS Lossiemouth.

We were kept away from the Wafus, who lived in nice new accommodation blocks with just four bods to a room.

Our mess was situated on the outskirts of the airfield, as far away from the galley, the Naafi and the bar as they could get us. It seems we tended to spread some form of bad influence if we were allowed to get too close.

Oh, and they said we drank too much... tut, tut.

So, they bundled us into old Nissan style brick huts, each had one antiquated coal burning stove in the centre which threw out just enough heat to take the chill off, but not stop the windows icing up on the inside.

When it got really cold, say during the winter, we stayed fully clothed and often in bed, wrapping the blankets and counterpanes around ourselves, or we stayed on watch.

One day I recall, the cooks had just finished cleaning away, the next watch were getting ready, the rest of us sat idly around the stove, reading the papers, chewing the fat, spinning dits as such when there was a huge explosion. Shit, snot and ash flew everywhere. Talk about shitting one's kegs, we thought we had been bombed, or a Buccaneer had crashed into our mess.

Total panic ensued, at least for a few minutes.

It turns out our ash bucket exploded because some knobhead chucked their empty can of shaving foam into the hot ash pan and the bloody thing popped, sending a cloud of ash and crap all over the mess.

It took us weeks to clean the place from top to toe so we could pass the CO's rounds.

No one admitted to being the plonker, but surely you can put your hands up now?

PEP-ME-UP PILLS

While in the mob, I got into a bit of a downer.

Now, back then mental health issues were seldom taken seriously; you were more often in line to get trooped for swinging the lead than treated.

Luckily, I was given some pills from the ships Doc to treat my total lack of interest and 'couldn't give a shit' attitude. Often called the NAFFI syndrome. (*No Ambition and Fuck all Interest*).

The pills did fuck all for me, but what did brighten my day was the instructions on the label.

It said, *"Take Two (2) tablets a day and you will be springing around like a marine in a gay bar in no time"*.

Seen in Tokyo hotel

Guests are requested not to smoke or do other disgusting behaviours in bed .

KING KONG WAS NOT WRONG

At Whale Island, training for the visit of the King & Queen of Greece.

The parade ground subby, referred to as 'King Kong' was giving it the final inspection before going up to the smoke.

I heard footsteps, they stopped right behind me.

A voice asked, "Who cut your fucking hair?"

I breathed a sigh of relief, thank fuck the question was not directed at me.

"A barber up the line, Sir."

"What did he cut it with, a fucking knife and fork?"

It was all I could do to hold it together.

NOTICE IN THE WINDOW OF DRY CLEANERS, BANGKOK

DROP YOUR TROUSERS HERE FOR THE BEST RESULTS.

THE FINAL INSPECTION

The Sailor stood and faced his God,

Which must always come to pass.

He hoped his shoes were shining,

Just as shiny as his brass

Step forward now you Navy Man,

How shall I deal with you?

Have you always turned the other cheek?

To My Church, have you been true?"

The sailor squared his shoulders and said,

"No, Lord, I guess I ain't.

Because those of us who shoot the guns,

Can't always be a saint.

I've had to work 'most every day,

And at times my talk was tough.

And sometimes I've been violent,

Because the world and sea is rough.

But I never took a penny,

That wasn't mine to keep...

Though I worked a lot of overtime,

When the bills got just too steep.

And I never passed a cry for help,

Though at times I shook with fear.

And sometimes, God, forgive me,

I've wept unmanly tears.

I know I don't deserve a place,

Among the people here.

They never wanted me around,

Except to calm their fears.

If you've a place for me here, Lord,

It needn't be so grand.

I never expected or had too much,

But if you don't, I'll understand.

There was a silence all around the throne,

Where the saints had often trod.

As the Navy Man waited quietly,

For the judgment of his God.

"Step forward now, you Sailor,

You've borne your burdens well.

Walk peacefully on Heaven's streets,

You've done your time in Hell."

AFTERWORD

Once again, we come to the end of a book.

It is a shame but this volume of Jacks Dits must conclude here.

But never fear; with hundreds of men and women serving on the ships of the grey funnel line, you can bet that, right now, right at this very moment, somewhere in the world there is a 'Jack' in some far-flung port, on some messdeck, or in some backstreet bar who is spinning a dit.

They will have a mug of Nato-Standard, or a Khai, or a cold glass of John Collins, maybe a Tiger beer, the bottle dripping with condensation, or a large Rum clasped in their sweaty paw.

For us old salts, there is a certain comfort knowing there will always be another dit to be told, another yarn to be spun, a ditty to be sung longer and louder than the last, one more Zulu warrior to chant, and more musical instruments for the music man who comes from down your way to play, more chariots coming over Jordan, shaggier dogs to groan at, and blacker cats to black cat the black catters.

And long may it continue to be so.

Paul [Knocker] White.

ABOUT THE AUTHOR

Paul White joined the Royal Navy in May 1973 (D139), as a six-week wonder boy out of Raleigh. A decade later, he was standing outside of Vicky Barracks making (the proverbial) rude signs at the Joss.

He has now lived in East Yorkshire for over thirty years.
Paul says, *"In another thirty years I expect I shall no longer be considered a newcomer."*

He is a multi-genre author of fiction, semi-fiction and non-fictional works. He is the founder of Electric Eclectic, an international alliance of independent authors, and of the Authors Professional Cooperative. He is the Editor-in-chief of Electric Press Literary Insights magazine.

Paul is an ardent independent traveller. He says, *"Those wild geese have never stopped calling"*.

He can often be found wandering around some far-flung location… or Scotland.
He is a nature lover and a supporter of ecological and wildlife preservation.
He says he has a *"warped sense of humour, is a lover good food, good wine and great company."*

Visit Paul's website

THE AUTHOR, PAUL - HMS RALEIGH, 1973

NAVAL SOCIAL HISTORY BOOKS

JACK'S DITS
TALL TALES FROM THE MESS
Original volume - Paperback only

THE PUSSERS COOKBOOK
TRADITIONAL ROYAL NAVY RECIPIES
Revised edition - Paperback & eBook

THE ANDREW, JACK & JENNY
ROYAL NAVY NICKNAMES, ORIGIN AND HISTORY
Paperback only

NEPTUNE & THE POLLYWOGS
Produced in conjunction with the Royal Navy Research Archives

DOCUMENTING THE TRADITIONAL ROYAL NAVY'S CROSSING THE LINE CEREMONY
Paperback only

HMS TIGER
CHRONICLES OF THE LAST BIG CAT
A4 Hardcover, only available from the author's website

SEMI-FICTION (military, not Naval)
LIFE IN THE WAR ZONE
PERSONAL STORIES BASED ON TRUE ACCOUNTS
Paperback Only

Visit Paul's Amazon Page

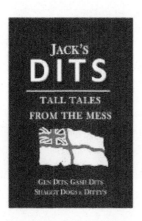

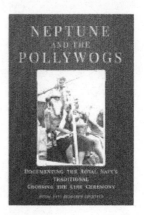

Printed in Great Britain
by Amazon

72232013R00119